Turning Up Roses

a Crestfield Inn Romance

Elsie Davis

I0694408

Sweet Romance Publishing

Cover Design by getcovers.com

Edited by Elaine Hyatt (Clarity Editing Services), & Beth Hale (Magnolia Author Services)

Sweet Romance Publishing

Sweetromancepublishing.com

PO Box 778

Liberty, NC 27298

TURNING UP ROSES

Proverbs 3: 5-6

Trust in the LORD with all your heart and lean not on your own understanding; in all your ways submit to him, and he will make your paths straight.

Chapter One

ANGELA PICKED UP AN orange, lifted it to her nose, and inhaled the citrusy scent. Images of Florida, warm sunshine, and fresh-squeezed orange juice filled her with a sense of renewed calm. Florida was her favorite vacation spot because of the amazing beaches and abundant saltwater sea life. The orange juice, on the other hand, was a favorite memory she held on to of her grandmother.

Isabella Carruthers enjoyed her juice every morning, the vibrant yellow-orange color a striking contrast to the white dishes and tablecloth she set out for breakfast. Angela had many such memories that she kept close in her heart, making her grandmother's absence seem less painful, and less lonely.

It was Isabella who taught Angela the art of perfumery. After her mother died when Angela was twelve, she'd gone to live with her grandmother, and the daily training of her olfactory senses had begun. Orange, plum, berry, vanilla, and earthy tobacco were some of her favorite fragrances. For years the two of them had worked on cultivating the perfect rose that would allow Angela to combine them into a unique formula.

Isabella once told her the key to success was to be unique in the perfume business. Which meant three things; having a good nose and the ability to pick out the different notes as they released into the air, the ability and knowledge to understand the chemistry in combining hundreds of various essential oils and scents, and the ability to be patient.

The patience part had always been the worst for Angela as a young girl. But life had a cruel way of fixing her impatient side.

For the umpteenth time, she wished her grandmother were with her now. Maybe then she wouldn't be so nervous about the competition. The first order of business had been to explore Cedar Grove, Vermont—home of the Jaranda Artisan Perfumery Contest. When she'd spotted the fresh food market, she hadn't been able to resist stopping in. The extensive fruit and produce offerings kept her shopping much longer than the grab-and-dash planned.

She added several oranges to her cart before moving to the next display of pineapples artfully arranged in rows. Angela reached for one of the spiny fruits, aiming for a golden-yellow one that would have a better chance of being ripe. Her hand collided with another customer's hand as they both reached for the same pineapple.

"Excuse me," she said, letting her gaze slide to his face. "I believe this is my pineapple." It was a stupid thing to say but staring at the man's chocolate brown eyes and handsome face, she said the first thing that came to mind.

"I disagree." He grinned. "I believe my hand touched it first," the man said, a glint of humor in his eyes. "And in Vermont, possession is nine-tenths of the law."

"I think that's countrywide, but I really had my heart set on this one. You see, it's got the greenest leaves, the sharpest points, the prettiest color, and of course, it's the largest. Oh, and it's for my sick mother," she added teasingly, grinning ear to ear as she joined in the fun.

"Well, in that case..." he drawled, "if it's about you getting your heart's desire *and* for a sick mother, I concede." He laughed, releasing the pineapple to her.

"A gentleman. Nice. And thank you. You do realize there's no sick mother, and I made the rest up," she confessed, not willing to let the falsehood stand.

"I do." The corners of his eyes crinkled as his smile deepened. "But as you said, I'd like to think I'm a gentleman. Just make sure you smell it first. Never judge a fruit by its cover."

"Surely you mean color."

She held the stem close to her nose and inhaled the sweet fragrance. Perfect, just as she knew it would be. "Thank you then, kind sir. I accept the pineapple with gratitude."

"Cover is a better word, don't you think? It applies to the stem, the spines, the color, the leaves—the whole package." His expression was serious, but the deep grooves in his cheekbones belied the smile he was trying to hide.

The man was flirting with her, plain and simple. Too bad she didn't live in Cedar Grove. Or maybe it was better that she *didn't* live here. Tall, attractive, clean-cut, and dressed in a pair of linen slacks, a dress shirt, and tie—everything about him proclaimed him a businessman. But it was his gentle smile and eyes that told her so much more. He was a genuinely nice guy. One who shopped in open-food markets—and knew his fruit. "Clearly, you know your way around a pineapple. I stand corrected."

"Spoken by the woman who knows the better end of a pineapple to smell. Equally impressive." The man picked up another pineapple, sniffing the bottom before adding it to his cart. "Have an enjoyable day," he said, angling his cart as if to go around hers and continue down the aisle. Coming abreast of her, he slowed, then stopped. "Your fragrance? What is it?" he asked.

"Why?" Angela was taken aback by the inquiry. Fruit was one thing; her own personal signature fragrance was another. She'd created the perfume years ago and still wore it every day. Angela loved it—not as much as the one recently finished, but close. She didn't dare wear the new one anywhere. Not after the last disastrous mistake that ended her potential to gain the necessary schooling to break into the perfume business and to be taken seriously. Naiveté would not be her downfall this time around.

"It's breathtaking. The fragrance seems vaguely familiar to me, but I can't remember the name." The man leaned closer, closing his eyes, and he drew another breath.

"Sounds to me like you date far too many women if you're into playing *name that fragrance*," she teased, pleased by his comment. *Breathtaking*. Her heart did a somersault. Angela couldn't remember the last time she felt comfortable flirting with someone, for her silly comment was all too obvious. It had to be the air of hope and expectation with which she had arrived in Cedar Grove for the competition.

"No worries on that score. Too busy to date, but I do enjoy an aromatic fragrance that leaves one wanting to know more. You too, or so it would seem, have a penchant for teasing the aromatic senses."

"Are you for real?" she asked, laughing. Guys didn't talk like that...unless...he was here for the same reason she was. The sobering thought landed with a thud. "Let me guess, you're here for the perfume competition. Are you an entrant or a judge?"

"Neither," he answered, his facial expression saying otherwise as lines of tension etched deeper into his brow. "What about you?" he countered.

"I'm in town on business," she said, her guard firmly in place as she preferred to sidestep the issue. She didn't want to lie, but there was no way she was telling him the truth. And technically, she *was* here on business. The business of winning a competition, collecting the prize money of twenty-five-thousand dollars, and a chance to work with a secret client to produce her fragrance into a marketable product.

This would be her chance to prove herself in the industry and put a checkered past behind her—finally. The past wasn't of her own doing unless you counted dating and trusting the wrong guy, but it was one that had ruined her chances at breaking into the perfume business four years ago.

"And the perfume?" he pressed, his frown deepening. "I pride myself on remembering ones that leave an impression."

"I don't remember the name. Orange Blossom, or something like that." She shrugged, hoping to change the subject. The orange was an easily identified note and wouldn't give away any pertinent details. Like the fact the orange was from a rose and carried the middle and base notes rather than the normal citrusy top notes one first smelled when spraying on a fragrance.

He nodded, not looking overly convinced. "Since you're here on business, as am I, would you care to have dinner with me?" His offer came as a surprise.

The bad part, however, was that she found it tempting—just not promising. Angela needed to keep her priorities straight, no matter how much she enjoyed talking to him. "Sorry. I'm busy this evening. Besides, I don't go on dinner dates with anyone I just met in the market," she teased, trying to ease the rejection.

"Fair enough. Have a nice day," he said, shooting her a gentle smile before continuing on his way down the aisle.

It would have been nice to go with the flow for once and say yes as a spur-of-the-moment decision. But dating and relationships had long ago been added to the don'ts column of her life rule's list. Justin Lockwood had seen to that with his deception. He'd not only stolen her formula and broken her heart, but his lies had cost her the future she should have had in the perfume industry. It had taken years to realize she hadn't really loved him—more like in love with the idea of being in love. She'd learned a hard but valuable lesson—don't trust people.

And it was also the reason she went by Angela Bradbury now instead of Lindsey. Angela was her middle name and had been an easy switch for her at the time. No one would connect her name with the fraudulent charges that had been levied against her and never proven, but that got her fired. The firing was like an unofficial confirmation, and doors at every perfumery had been closed to her.

Grant paid for his produce and left the market, but he couldn't stop thinking about the woman—or her fragrance. The scent was uncannily like one he knew, but Orange Blossom certainly wasn't the name. More like something French, the mixture of orange and vanilla a unique spring-like fragrance. It was like capturing a summer breeze. And on the woman, the scent was better than he remembered.

It wasn't one of Jaranda's fragrances, that much he knew for sure.

Jaranda's perfumes were some of the finest in the world, but then the company had been in his family for over sixty years, and his grandfather had spared no expense when he opened the experimental labs and manufacturing plants. Grant was the sole heir after his father died in a car accident. Unfortunately, he would be the last of the Edward's family and the family-owned business as it was known today because marriage and family were not on his agenda.

At some point, he needed to set up a trust for the company to ensure its continuance was managed in a way suitable to the family values. But for now, his focus was on something entirely different—a new signature fragrance for Jaranda. Something to take the world of women and elegance to a new level. Only Alan, his second in command and Vice President of Operations, knew Grant was the secret client behind the competition.

The brief the contestants were given served as a guideline for what the client wanted, giving them a chance to create and formulate their best offering over the course of the past two months. Only three of those samples would make it to the client as finalist entries. The decision would be based on the fragrance, and the ability of the entrant to think and create on their feet—proof they were up to the task on their own merits. The method would separate the advanced perfumers from the beginners and from the lucky.

And if Grant intended to get a fair assessment of the competitors and their abilities to make the right decision for the company, it was paramount they see him only as the owner of Jaranda—not as the client.

He returned to the Crestfield Inn, a French colonial bed and breakfast he'd stayed at once before and enjoyed enough that it swayed his decision with where to hold the competition. "Good afternoon, Kyle," Grant called out when he spotted the guy at the front desk bent over his computer and deep in thought.

"Hey there. I see you found the fresh market okay," Kyle said, eyeing the bag he carried.

"I did. Popular place. Have the others arrived yet?" Grant asked.

Kyle clicked a few keys on the computer. "Two checked in about an hour ago. Would you like me to let you know when the third arrival checks in?"

Grant shook his head. "No, that's okay. I'll meet with all the judges in the morning. They can enjoy their first night out in Cedar Grove. Starting tomorrow, they will have their hands full as the first round of the competition takes place."

"Sounds good. This is an exciting event for the town as we've never had anything like a fragrance competition. And to think, top perfumers from all over the world will be in the area, and after tomorrow, all staying here at the Crestfield Inn. Mr. Montpelier was thrilled you chose us." Kyle beamed; the man's excitement echoed in his enthusiastic response.

"I stayed here once before and fell in love with the idyllic setting, of both the inn and the town. The logistics had to be worked out seeing as it's a small town with limited lodging choices." A couple of cancellations at the inn had moved Grant toward finalizing those plans once he realized he could fit all the first-round finalists into one place.

"Can anyone go to the competition and watch the first round?" Kyle asked. "People around town have been asking and are definitely planning on showing up."

"They can, but it won't be easy to see. They'll be set up in booths at the park, so they can only wander around and check things out from a distance. Luckily, the weather is cooperating. Liberty Park was the only place I could set up fifty booths and spread them out in a way as to afford privacy to each of the contestants as they create." Alan had been instrumental in helping him coordinate everything. Unfortunately, his VP had to remain behind at the office while Grant handled the competition with a behind-the-scenes attitude.

"I bet that was a design nightmare."

"Yes, but shelter canopies did the privacy trick, which also gave us some protection against the elements if Mother Nature hadn't cooperated. And once the eight finalists move into the inn, you, my friend, will be busy." It had been a tight fit, but the twelve rooms available for lodging had been the perfect number for what he needed.

"Will you be dining in the Garden Delight tonight? You should make a reservation if you are," Kyle reminded him.

"No, I'm thinking of going over to Cade's Tavern. Plenty of other nights moving forward that the group will dine together here at the inn. I'll get some privacy while I can." Grant chuckled.

"Then have a nice night if I don't see you again. And of course, let me know if there's anything I can do for you or get you. I'm happy to help."

"Thanks, Kyle. I'll do that. Good night."

Grant headed up the stairs to his room, choosing to sit in the oversized antique armchair positioned by the window. It was his favorite view, overlooking the gardens from the third floor of the inn—the view a reminder of his mother's garden. She'd spent painstaking but loving hours on her flowers and bushes, right up until she got sick and passed away. Watching her tend her roses was one of his favorite pastimes.

After laying out a towel to protect the table, he cut up the pineapple with his pocketknife. No good boy scout was ever without one, and it was something that came in handy quite often.

The image of the woman at the market came to mind as he took his first bite, savoring the delicious flavor bursting in his mouth. Sweet and zingy, just like the brunette. It was a shame she had turned him down for dinner, as the evening would have been way more interesting. She was easy to talk to, and he enjoyed her teasing comebacks.

And they were both visiting Cedar Grove, which made their situation perfect. He wasn't a fan of relationships and marriage, but that didn't mean he avoided women all together. Just any semblance of permanency that would give a woman the chance to destroy your trust—like Amanda had done to him. His ex-wife had taught him a life lesson he wasn't soon to forget.

His family had been right about Amanda from the start...she had been after money.

Chapter Two

IT WAS A SHORT drive to the neighboring town of Willow Springs. Cedar Grove didn't have enough motel rooms available to house the fifty contestants, the judges, and all the other officials needed for this event, and Angela had been assigned to one of the overflow motels.

After checking in, she spent the rest of the day mentally reviewing the rules of the contest, and of course, going over and over the formula for her sample. To her, it was perfect, but what if it could be better? Her grandmother would have known, her instincts for artisan perfuming well known in the industry. They called it a gift.

She hadn't cashed in on her grandmother's name, preferring to establish a reputation in the industry on her own. In hindsight, it might have been a mistake, but still, Angela didn't want to ride on the coattails of her mentor.

The prize money and the accolades that came with winning this contest would go a long way to assuaging her injured reputation and pride. By the time evening rolled around, she forced herself to head out to dinner for a quick bite, wanting to be well-rested for tomorrow. Driving through the town, she spotted Angela's Steakhouse and opted for more than fast food. *God's divine intervention perhaps?* With a name like that—the place had to be good.

Angela shook her head, amused by her train of thought. God had far more important things on him mind than where she ate dinner. And there was obviously no such guarantee the food would be palatable, but it was as good as any other method she could use to pick from the local restaurants.

"Good evening and welcome to Angela's," the host greeted her, a friendly smile on his face. "Will someone be joining you for dinner, or is this dinner for one?" It was a question she hated.

"Dinner for one." Always one—and had been for a long time. It was like wearing a scarlet letter "A" on her forehead. *Alone. Available. Approachable.*

The man led her to a table for two, of course. They always did—so why ask? He held her chair out, placing a napkin over her lap after she sat and got comfortable. "Here's the menu," he said, handing her the unfolded supersized printout of tonight's specials. "Every night, the selections are handpicked based on seasonal offerings, and of course, our signature steaks." The host poured her a glass of water from the pitcher on the table. "If you have any questions, your server, Melissa, will be over in a minute to answer."

"Thank you." He was very thorough in his responsibilities, even managing to pick up the second place setting before he walked away. At least it didn't look like she was being stood up, she chuckled to herself. *Like eating alone was any better.*

The menu offered amazing choices, which made the decision difficult. Her server hadn't shown up right away, which was fine. It gave her a chance to look around and scope out the place. There were only a handful of dinner guests, as the evening was still early. Angela's gaze landed on a lone figure sitting at a table by the window. The telltale single place setting announced he was in the same position as she was—dining alone.

The man turned to flag his server, and Angela recognized him as the man from the fresh market this morning. If he hadn't been here first, she would have worried he was stalking her. The odds were slim to none of another chance meeting. She had meant what she told him about being too busy, but it was her lack of trust that had her slouching back against the cushion, not wanting to be recognized.

Her server approached. "Good evening, ma'am. Sorry it took a little longer to get over here. Before I answer any questions you have about the menu, the gentleman over there," she paused and pointed toward the table in the front window, "is asking if you'd like to join him for dinner as he's only just arrived. Claims he met you this morning."

Angela didn't bother looking to where the server pointed, knowing who was there. And as to *met this morning*, that was a bit of a stretch—more like bumped into each other. It was on the tip of her tongue to refuse, but she hesitated. What harm could come from a chance meeting at a restaurant? He wasn't a mind reader and hadn't known she would come here. It was a chance to dine at a nice restaurant with a nice man, no strings attached.

"Seems like a good guy, if you ask me," the server said as if recognizing her hesitation.

"Okay, I'll do it." It was just one meal, not a commitment to anything else.

The woman smiled. "You go on ahead. I'll bring your table setting and get you set right up."

Angela took a deep breath and headed for his table. She didn't even know his name, for Pete's sake. He glanced her way, his warm gaze reminding her of their friendly banter this morning. It helped check her racing heart just enough to keep her moving forward, as the thought of dinner with a stranger hadn't sat well.

Standing as she approached, he reached out a hand. "Hi, thanks for not making me eat dinner alone tonight," he said, smiling as he enfolded her hand in his. Name's Grant Edwards, by the way."

The name Grant Edwards vaguely rang a bell, but then Edwards was a common enough name. She certainly hadn't met the guy, his handsome face and classic good looks not something a woman would easily forget. "Hi, and thanks for the offer. My name's Angela Bradbury."

Grant's brow drew tight, not much, but just enough for her to notice. And worry. This could be another mistake on her part.

"It's nice to meet you, officially." His smile had returned, making her second guess what she saw.

"I agree. Mr. Pineapple Man seems so out there," she teased, trying to relax. They were in a public place, so that in itself was safe enough.

"By that comment, does it mean you've thought about me today, as well?" Her heart raced a little faster, not only because she had, but because he was admitting he'd thought about her.

"Don't flatter yourself. It's what I thought when I put a face to the dinner invitation," she lied.

Grant sat back in his seat and nodded. "I see. Well, I've thought of you, or your fragrance that is." He winked, shooting her a grin. "Orange Blossom isn't right though."

Another clue this was dangerous territory. Grant was hung up on her perfume—her own personal fragrance and one he couldn't have smelled before unless they'd met previously. Something she established earlier that wasn't likely. What if he was a competitor?

Tonight's meeting was by chance...and she'd see it through, but perfumes and the competition were off-limits as discussion topics.

Totally.

Surprised to see the woman he'd met earlier today at the fresh market in the same restaurant for dinner. Grant's curiosity prompted an invitation for her to join him. She'd turned down the offer to dine together this morning, but sitting in the same restaurant, both alone, it seemed slightly on the ridiculous side not to reissue the invite. It would give him another chance to find out about the perfume, but more importantly, it would break the boredom of another lonely evening and talking to himself for entertainment.

Not that he actually talked out loud, but he did go over every aspect of the business. Repeatedly. The family business had always been successful, but sales had been sluggish the past six months. It had been enough of a slump to prompt him to devise the competition. A new fragrance that would take the world by storm was the perfect solution.

His first request to spend time with her had been solely based on an opportunity to be normal, and for once, forget about business. The second he recognized her name; Grant regretted the invite. Three seconds later, he recognized it as the perfect opportunity to get to know her without the added guise of pretense once his identity was discovered.

He planned to get to know the final contestants, and there was no guarantee Angela would be amongst them. Luckily, he wasn't one of the judges. There was no off-handed chance of anyone claiming foul play by two strangers having dinner together. And to be on the safe side, there would be no business discussions.

"Did you order yet?" Angela asked, glancing down at the menu.

He nodded. "I did, but I asked them to hold up on putting it in until I knew if you'd be joining me."

"Thanks, that was sweet of you. Must have been the pineapple you ate." Her shiny, pink-tinged lips were pulled back into a broad smile—the expression "kissable lips" coming to mind. "Mine was deliciously sweet, bold, and quite juicy."

It was dinner, not a date, something he needed to remember. "Mine was equally delicious. If I would have been quicker on my feet, I'd have asked you to share a pineapple with me since we had the same penchant for one." There was nothing wrong with teasing, on the other hand.

"Except you would have gotten the same response as your other offer." Angela took a sip of water and laid down her menu.

"*Hmmm*. I seem to remember I was rejected, but here I am, sitting with you. A pleasant change to the course of the evening."

Angela laughed. "It's not what I expected, but as to pleasant, I will withhold judgment until after dinner. What did you order?" she asked, changing the subject. "I'm having a tough time choosing."

"Fair enough. I ordered the fresh Atlantic salmon on special, with a touch of ginger spice." Originally, he'd planned on going to Cade's Tavern, but he'd seen the online specials posted for Angela's and changed his destination. Besides, he'd also figured there was less opportunity to run into anyone he knew. So much for that idea, but the result was more than satisfactory.

"That sounds yummy." It was her fresh, laid-back attitude that appealed him. No airs and graces like those of Amanda.

The server approached, arranging Angela's place setting before she topped off their waters. "I've got the white Sauvignon Blanc you ordered coming right up," she said, shooting him a quick glance before turning to Angela. "Do you have any questions, or do you know what you'd like to order?" she asked, pen and pad at the ready.

"I'll order. I was going to have the salmon, but I can't resist the house special for a juicy steak dinner. Medium rare, please. Broccoli and mashed potatoes as my sides."

"Good choice, trust me. Would you like some wine also? I can bring you a glass, or if you prefer red, we have several good selections that would pair well with your steak." Melissa leaned forward and pointed to the list of wines on the bottom of the back page of the menu.

"The white will be fine. Thank you. I'm not that much of a wine drinker, so it's all the same to me." Angela smiled, handing the server back the menu.

Grant sat back in his chair, admiring his dinner date after the server left. Medium-length light blonde hair danced in the candlelight as she moved, her fair complexion glowing. Graceful slender fingers wrapped around her water glass tightly, as if she were nervous. But it was her deep green eyes that entranced him, the shade unusual and yet, not one easily forgotten. They were like emeralds in the moonlight. "So, why don't we start by you telling me about yourself." He figured it would be easier to steer the conversation if he led it.

"There's not much to tell. I work at a coffee shop as a barista, live in New Jersey, and my family is my church family. Otherwise, I'm on my own."

He already knew some of her answers to the question, having reviewed every application repeatedly—hers more than once. Angela had zero experience and was doing nothing to enhance her resume as a perfumer, and he'd been hard-pressed to pick her application. In fact, she was his last choice for the fifty chosen to attend the competition.

"I see. So what's a Jersey girl barista doing in Cedar Grove?" She hadn't even had any specialized training other than collaborating with a grandmother, which didn't come highly rated in this business. But it was her essay answer that kept him coming back to consider her. Poetic and flowing, the words called to him in a way he could almost smell the fragrance on the young girl she'd described running through the meadow. Her lack of experience in the perfume industry was made up for in her poetic justice of the use of the English language to describe the perfume in a way to make one feel, not just smell. Perhaps her flowery description and the emotion conveyed was the result of her being on her own, Grant more than a little curious about her backstory.

She looked uncomfortable with his direct question, and he sensed Angela would be reluctant to discuss anything deeper than standard get-to-know you conversation.

"I'd rather not talk about business tonight. I get enough of it all day. What if we both simply agree to talk about anything but business? Then we can relax and enjoy the evening."

Grant liked the sound of it a lot. "Sounds perfect. Business does tend to be all-consuming." It made things easy for him, but what of her? Why the secrecy? Business was a safe subject for most people. It was like her perfume—both an enigma. Good thing problem solving was one of his specialties. "So, if not business, let's talk about everything else."

"We can ask each other questions...but nothing about work, or too personal." She smiled and nodded, falling in line with the direction the evening had taken.

Enough so, Grant could almost feel her tension dissipate. He realized he was looking forward to their non-date date, and for once, simply enjoying the company of a woman. *No strings attached.*

Chapter Three

WAKING UP AS THE first slivers of daylight slid past the damask drapes, Angela rolled out of bed, nervous anticipation radiating through every pore of her body. Last night with Grant had been enjoyable, the two of them discussing everything from favorite foods to favorite fun activities and hobbies. She couldn't remember the last time she'd had so much fun. Once they'd tabled any discussion of business, she'd loosened up and taken the companionship at face value—a one-off event that helped her while away the evening instead of nervously pacing her room all night.

But dinner with Grant was in the past, and today was the next step in a line of many to move closer to her end goal. She had to make it through the first round of cutoffs. Each step would become more difficult, but it would drive her crazy to worry about them. They hadn't even announced what today's challenge consisted of, but Angela was sure it would be a doozy. Some of the best perfumers in the world would be vying for the notoriety that would be bestowed upon them if they won. For Angela, it was so much more.

It was her future.

She picked up the portfolio of information she'd received in the mail after she'd been selected as a finalist. The congratulatory letter included details about her check-in and the general process from here on out. Round one started promptly at nine at Liberty Park in Cedar Grove, and check-in started at eight-thirty, where she would receive her booth number and her instructions for this part of the contest. At the end of the round, the judges would announce the results by three p.m. From there, the eight finalists selected would all move to the Crestfield Inn in Cedar Grove, where they and the judges would stay during the final two rounds for as long as they were in the running.

It was like a reality TV show, where you stayed until you were booted off, or out in this case. Only it was her own reality and not a case of looking in from the outside. Angela took a deep breath and glanced at her watch. She'd leave in an hour to be on the safe side, preferring to be in the vicinity of the park plenty early. She grabbed an orange, peeled it, inhaling the fresh scent to help calm her nerves. The bursting flavor lit up her mouth and helped to clear her head. Next stop, a hot shower and her favorite body wash. Aromatherapy was the ticket to calm her inner soul—something her grandmother had taught her to awaken her senses to the possibilities in life.

###

By eight-fifteen, Angela arrived at the park, finding it difficult to locate a parking spot. Two blocks weren't exactly close, but she grabbed the first available one, not daring to spend time to drive around again in the hopes of getting something better. She pressed in the clutch and shifted into reverse, backing into the space slowly. Managing to get it right on the first try, she pulled slightly forward, locked the doors, and pocketed her keys.

As she drew closer to the park, the amount of activity increased. Inside, there were lots of people milling about the registration table with the same idea of an early check-in. She moved into the line with several others, glancing around, but of course, recognizing no one. There was row after row of booths set up, like a craft fair. At least she wouldn't feel as though the other contestants were watching her every move. Privacy came high on her priority list and with good reason.

"Good morning, I'm Angela Bradbury," she said, smiling at the elderly woman checking everyone in. Inside, she was nervous as a tick, but she didn't want to let her inexperience show.

"Good morning. I've got you right here," the woman said, crossing her name off a list. She picked up a packet and handed it to Angela. "Here is your information regarding the first round. You're free to open the packet and look them over because there's no advantage or disadvantage to reading them earlier than the others. The final piece that counts won't be revealed until the contest starts." The woman's friendly smile gave her a tiny bit of reassurance, calming at least three of the hundreds of butterflies fluttering around in her stomach.

"Thank you." She glanced at the envelope in her hand and back at the woman as she handed Angela her name badge and a number card. Her heart sank when she saw the number she'd been assigned.

"You're in booth thirteen. Please make sure you're there at least fifteen minutes before the nine a.m. start as this is a timed event. The clock starts for everyone."

"Sounds good. I'll go there now and try to relax. Not that I think it will be of much use." She aimed for a smile, but the best she could muster was a light-hearted one as she nervously bit her lower lip.

"Good luck to you," the woman said, something Angela was sure she told everyone. But of all the perfumers here, she felt as though she needed it the most. She was probably the only one here without a degree in chemistry, or a high-falutin' job in the perfume industry, or an expert perfumer with a track record. And now, she had drawn the number thirteen.

"Thanks," she said, walking away to find her booth, anxious to read the instructions regardless of what the woman said. She might not know what the final details were, but surely, it would give her some tiny hint as to what lay ahead.

Angela found the white shelter with a small sign indicating it was booth thirteen. "Good morning. This is me," she said, showing the attendant her pass.

He nodded, stepping aside to let her enter. "Good morning. My name's Jerry, and I'm your contest coordinator for the day. If you need anything, just ask, and I'll do my best to help you out. Your worktable is locked, and I'll be in to open it at nine sharp, when the round officially begins. Until then, try to relax. And congratulations for making it this far." His warm smile was intended to put her at ease, but nothing could shake the fluttering in her belly.

"Thank you, Jerry. It's crazy to be here, and nothing will help me to relax—other than getting this round over with, that is." She shook her head and shrugged.

As she entered the booth, Jerry let the flaps close behind her, and she was left alone to investigate. Just as he said, there was a large table in the center, but the cover prevented her from gathering any clues about what was ahead. The chair looked comfortable, which was a huge plus, depending on how long they'd be at their assigned task.

Off to the side was another smaller table, laid out with water, juice, soda, and snacks. She moved to the table to get a bottle of water, returning to the desk to sit, intent on reading the packet of information.

Angela slid out the instructions.

Good morning everyone,

Thanks for joining us as finalist, and we wish every one of you the best of luck in round one. By now, you've met your coordinator. Feel free to reach out to them if you have any questions. This round starts promptly at nine. At that time, your coordinator will unlock the table and the secrets within. All contestants will have the same fragrance oils and the same amount of time to create their entry in today's competition. There will be a card on the table to explain your task, and again, everyone has the same card.

Patience is a virtue in perfuming, but this is a timed event, so you will need to throw that rule out of your repertoire and rely more on instinct. You will have until noon to complete the assignment. We will break for lunch and enjoy a short get-together while the judges review the entries and decide on the eight finalists who will proceed to the next round, and of course, move to the Crestfield Inn.

Unfortunately, I'm not in attendance at the event, but as the overall contest coordinator, please let me know if there's anything I can do to assist you by emailing me or phoning me directly.

Alan Watkins
Vice President of Jaranda Perfumes
AW@Jaranda.com
802-203-2134

The woman at the registration table was spot on in her comment. The instructions told her what she needed to know except the most important detail—the assigned task. Another glance at her watch revealed there were only ten more minutes before she would find out anyway. Using the time wisely, she practiced her deep breathing, letting her senses open to everything that was around her in the tent.

Sharply at nine, Jerry stepped into the tent. "It's time to begin," he said, tying open the flaps. "I'll be here the whole time, just outside. The judges will be walking around, as well as a few monitors to keep an eye on the whole proceeding. They may occasionally step inside to observe. The client has asked that we use great care to make sure everyone abides by the rules. Any questions?"

"None that won't be answered in about thirty seconds," she said, laughing as he reached to unlock her table.

"You'll be fine. I'll give you warnings at the top of the hour at ten and eleven and then at ten minutes to noon. At that time, I will seal the vial you hand me, and then you'll sign the label identifying it as yours. After that, you wait for the judge's decisions to find out if you move on to the next round." He removed the cover and laid it on the ground.

"Gotcha," Angela said, reaching for the envelope, her hand shaking.

"You may begin. And good luck," Jerry said as he moved to position himself at the front of the tent.

"Thank you." She took a deep breath and slid an index card out of the envelope.

There are fifty essential oils at your disposal.

This round is designed to showcase your fundamental knowledge of fragrance. Awaken your senses and be creative, focusing on one word.

Memories...

Angela closed her eyes. *Please, Lord. Help me to focus my energies. Help me to feel rather than think about what I'm doing.* It sounded like a simple enough task, but she knew better than to hang on to the thought. *Dig deeper*—two of her grandmother's favorite instructional words came to mind.

Memories could mean anything. Emotionally charged events triggered them, but they could be anything from happy, love, and joy, to sad, pain, and sorrow. The list was endless. She glanced at the fifty oils, pausing at each bottle to register the scent and evoke the image she associated with it. Another of her grandmother's teaching points. Associate scents with the familiar for easy recall and a feeling attached to the fragrance. She knew most of the oils, but some she paused to remove the stopper, teasing her senses with only the barest hint of the oil so as not to overpower her nose or her brain with any one scent.

"It's ten o'clock," Jerry called out, startling her as he approached.

"Okay, thanks." Angela shook her head. Time had flown by, and she hadn't even started on the assigned task. Panic welled up within her. She'd been lost to the new fragrances and trying to mentally concoct an image for each one, and then went way beyond to fit in the feeling evoked. Winners had to excel, not just fit.

Jerry glanced down at the table and back at her. "Do you need anything?" He was aware she hadn't started yet, but it's not like he could help her with what she needed to figure out. A memory that expressed all emotion. Something that embraced the feelings of memories more than the memory itself.

That's it.

Memories evoked feelings, a rush of endorphins within the body, joy being the strongest. Memories are stored in the amygdala, and she needed a fragrance to mimic the stimulation of that special part of the brain—something to slow the heart rate and allow one to breathe, relax, and feel good.

Panic turned to excitement. "I'm good," Angela said, smiling up at him. She was confident she was on the right track and quickly went to work, blocking out all else around her. Going back through the fragrances, she carefully selected the ones she thought would pair well together. Two of the new-to-her fragrances were added to the mix, Angela curious enough to want to play with the possibilities.

Several vials were lined up in front of her as she changed up the formula in each one, pausing to label the oils and quantities she'd added. First the top notes, then the middle notes, and then the heart of the fragrance–the base notes.

Patchouli was a favorite for relaxation but required a more pleasing oil to soften the smell—something like lavender. Spearmint was another interesting choice, and although more stimulating, it still helped relax the respiratory and nervous system and release emotional blocks. She also played with some combinations using the expensive and new to her fragrance of Neroli; having read once that it supported healing of the mind, body, and spirit. There were a few others like Bergamot for balancing hormones, lemon for calming, and of course, rose for harmony—her favorite in almost any variation.

Two hours were spent mixing and remixing and sampling her creation on test strips until she was satisfied. Angela sat back, satisfied with her final fragrance compound. Letting out a deep breath of air, she took a sip of water.

"Time's up," Jerry said, stepping into the tent.

Angela hadn't heard his other time warnings, deep in thought, but this she heard. "Great. I'm finished." She held up her vial, making sure the stopper lid was tight before handing it to him.

Jerry added the seal and handed it back for her to sign. "Nicely done, and just in time."

"Close call, but then it took a bit for my inspiration to kick in," Angela said, smiling.

He took the vial from her and handed it to the judge who'd come to collect it. "Very close," he said, shaking his head. "When I saw you hadn't even started by ten, I'll admit I was nervous for you."

She nodded. "You weren't the only one."

"There's a luncheon buffet set up and plenty of places to eat. Feel free to meet and talk with some of the other contestants while we wait for the judge's decisions at three."

"Sounds good. I'm famished. I didn't eat much this morning because my stomach was in knots."

Angela made her way to the luncheon area. Fifty hopefuls, all eagerly awaiting the news and wanting to make it to the next round. What would they talk about when secretly they knew forty-two of them were going home?

Talk about stressful—but at least her part in the process was over. She was either moving to the next round or going home, but it was out of her hands at this point.

Chapter Four

PURPOSELY CHOOSING A TABLE the furthest away from the buffet area where most of the contestants stood talking and eating, Angela sat down. Questions about where she worked, what she created, and where she trained would be repeatedly asked, and her answers would only earn her disdainful looks, not friends.

She gazed around the area—people watching. It was something she'd learned to do when she was a child to pass the time. Now, she did it because she found it interesting—like Alice in Wonderland looking through a glass into a world Angela didn't fit into. *At least not yet anyway.*

This contest could change all that for her, and after four years of waiting for the right moment, she figured it was time to stand up and be counted or give up. At twenty-nine, she wasn't getting any younger, and it was past time to figure out what she was going to do with her life. Her goal all along had been to try and break into the business one last time. Just to say she'd given it her best shot.

The Jaranda Artisan Perfume competition had come at the perfect time, Angela considering it a sign. Thirty was just around the corner, and although she enjoyed being a barista, the aroma of freshly brewed coffee tripping some of her favorite olfactory senses—perfumes were her true passion.

One woman was talking, her animation reflected in hand gestures. Someone called to her and waved. The woman turned, her heel catching in the ground, and she stumbled. The man she'd been talking to shot forward to steady her, just as the woman's arm flailed upward, her plate of food flying the short distance it took to land squarely against the man's chest. He jumped back, brushing the food away and then shaking off his hands as he searched for what Angela assumed would be a napkin.

It had been like watching a humorous play in slow motion. Angela smiled. The poor unfortunate man had come up on the wrong end of the deal. Her gaze zeroed in on him, wondering how he was taking the fiasco. The man looked familiar. Disgustingly familiar. The blood pounded in her head as she tried to breathe.

Justin Lockwood. The man who stole her formula and ruined her life. Her hand shook as she pushed her hair off her face, trying to grasp this sudden twist. This couldn't be happening. A sense of déjà vu hit her, and not in a good way. She wanted to run and hide. Why, oh why, did he have to be here? He was no doubt a contestant, because with his sordid character, she couldn't imagine anyone would choose him to be a judge or coordinator. But then, maybe no one knew him as well as she did.

It's not as if she could leave, but what if he recognized her? His slimy smirk the last time she'd seen him was one that haunted her for four years. He'd been thrilled she'd gotten fired. Seeing him again brought back all the anger she'd managed to keep on lock-down.

Angela spent the rest of the afternoon avoiding Justin, managing to always stay far, far away. By three, she was worn out and ready to go back to her hotel. Running wasn't the answer—but fighting for what she believed, now that would work. She belonged here—and Justin didn't. Hopefully, after today he'd be long gone and back to the rock he had crawled out from under.

Unable to do anything about his presence, she had to focus on herself and holding her head up high. She'd force a cool exterior to the surface for all to see. Inside, however, she was trembling. Taking the initiative, she waltzed up to the front row and took a seat for the judge's announcements as they gathered on the small stage erected.

"Good afternoon, ladies and gentlemen," the speaker said into the mic, tapping it to make sure it was working. My name is Anthony Quint, and I'm one of the judges. With me tonight, and serving as judges for the competition, are Lacy Danvers and Grace Sanders." He pointed to each of the women next to him, and a round of applause erupted.

The buzz of talking ceased, and the contestants took their seats, the coordinators standing in the back to watch the proceedings. Several news cameramen were also present. Today's finalists would be on the five o'clock news. She was sure of it. How often did one see an international competition in a small New England town?

"First, let me thank you all for coming to Cedar Grove for this special event. We appreciate the extraordinary talent represented by what we considered the top fifty entrants into the competition. Unfortunately, this is the end of the line for many, but it is with huge applause as the other judges and I have had a difficult time narrowing this talented group of perfumers down to only eight finalists. So again, many thanks to all of you for making this into what promises to be an amazing competition. The talent pool present is incredible.

"So, without further ado, I'd like to announce the eight finalists. As I do, please come up and join me on the stage. I'd like to ask everyone to hold your applause until after all the names have been called. And on a side note, the names are being called in no particular order as the eight are not being ranked." The judges all stood side by side, smiling as they faced the group.

Angela closed her eyes. *Please, Lord, let them call my name.* One last prayer after many couldn't hurt.

"Congratulations to...Mark Witherspoon...Barbara Fanning...Heather Bullock... William Bartlett...Justin Lockwood..."

Justin made the finals. Angela couldn't believe it. This is not at all what she expected when she signed up. It wasn't fair. The man was a fake—a thief. She watched as he took his place on stage with the others. The room started to spin, images of the past flashing in her head, drowning out everything else around her.

The sound of clapping broke into her nightmarish images. Angela wanted to cry. She hadn't heard the rest of the names, but clearly, she wasn't one of them if everyone was clapping. The contest was over for her, and once again, Justin had beaten her out. But this time, she'd lost everything without his interference.

A sea of smiling faces up on the stage stared back at the crowd while a sea of raging torment crashed inside her. Angela stood, prepared to make a beeline exit, preferring to be alone, as she fought back her tears.

"Angela Bradbury are you still here?" the judge called out, stopping her in her tracks. He was calling her name, but why? She lifted her hand to let him know she was, using her other hand to shield her eyes against the stage lights as she tried to understand what was going on.

"Where are you going? The steps are over here." He chuckled, pointing toward the front and center stage area." He wanted her on stage.

She was a finalist.

The reality brought a fresh wave of tears to her eyes that she couldn't hold back, making it difficult to move. Her heart raced, the overwhelming joy incredible.

She'd made it. She'd made it. Thank you, Lord.

Angela took a step forward, and then another, until she was on the stage with the others, taking her place as far from Justin as she could manage. She'd deal with his presence later. For now, she wanted to bask in the joy of moving to the next round of the competition.

"Glad you could join us, Angela," the judge said, smiling. Laughter rippled through the crowd as another round of applause erupted.

###

Angela still couldn't believe she'd made the cut. Instead of packing to go home, she was packing to move to the Crestfield Inn. The fact Justin had also made it was the only negative in her joy. It wouldn't be easy, but she'd avoid him the same way she had at the luncheon. With any luck, he wouldn't recognize her.

Different name, different hairstyle. Not to mention, he'd only been interested in her formula, not her. By now, she'd be just another face in a lengthy line of many, she was certain. There'd been no look of recognition on stage, but then he'd been too busy gloating and patting himself on the back, his arrogant pride in overload.

As she drove toward the inn, her tension increased with each minute, causing her to miss a turn. She really needed to get a grip on her emotions. This was supposed to be fun—a happy, joyful moment in her life. Making it to the top eight would get her noticed by perfume companies when she added it to her resume. This was something that couldn't be taken away from her. At least, she hoped not, a tiny niggling of fear settling deep in her stomach. With Justin in the mix, one couldn't be too sure of anything. The man was a dark scoundrel without a lick of conscience.

Parking in the driveway next to the massive French Colonial mansion, she grabbed her suitcase and headed for the door. Rose bushes lined the edge of the lush lawn and lined the sidewalk that led to the front porch. She stopped to breathe in the luxurious fragrance lingering in the air, knowing it would help calm her. Roses had always been her favorite, which is why the special ingredient for her sample fragrance centered on a rose. Her very own unique, breathtaking, aromatic rose. Well, her grandmother's and hers.

Isabella's Honey Angel.

Together, they'd created a masterpiece, its velvety petals a soft yellow that mirrored the sun, its fragrance light and dreamy, like a walk through a honeysuckle meadow. Her grandmother had started crossbreeding roses, and from there, Angela had been fascinated and worked with her own cultivated varieties until her rose was perfection. She'd named it after her grandmother seeing as she started the original process, but it was more than that. It was Angela's way to honor the woman who had not only oversaw her training but had been like a mother to her. She liked to picture her grandmother watching over from heaven, guiding Angela forward now and giving her the courage needed.

The rose plants were kept under lock and key in her special greenhouse, and she'd told no one about what she was doing. Secrecy was key, a lesson she wasn't soon to forget. Even the perfume formula she had created for the contest had been logged in her journal and stored in a lockbox hidden under the floorboards of her bedroom.

Once she'd been satisfied with the rose, the long process of creating the perfect fragrance had begun. Zeroing in on the right amount of Isabella's Honey Angel oil had taken months and months of arduous work and failed attempts to create the dream fragrance she'd envisioned.

Which is why the timing for the Jaranda competition seemed like fate. She hadn't needed the two months they'd allocated for the contestants to design something to match the brief written by the confidential client. Her sample fragrance had already been finished. Now, all she had to do was be one of the lucky three in order to get her sample in front of the client.

She'd used the two months instead to make more, not that she dared to wear it in public. For that, she stuck to her original fragrance. The one she'd perfected—*after* Justin stole the basic formula.

Walking in, she was greeted with a friendly smile from the man behind the front desk.

"Welcome to the Crestfield Inn. I'm Kyle, front desk manager, and the anything-you-need, just-ask guy," he said, laughing as he pushed closed the file he'd been working on. His cheery attitude went a long way to easing her tension.

"Hi there. I'm Angela Bradbury, one of the finalists in the competition."

"Ah, yes. I've got your name right here," he said, pointing to his clipboard. "You've been assigned to room seven, second floor and to the left." He opened a drawer, pulled out a key, and handed it to her. "Here's your key. Congratulations on finaling, and I hope you'll enjoy your stay with us. Breakfast and lunch are served daily in the Garden Delight Bistro down the hall in that direction. It can be found at the back of the inn, where it overlooks an incredible flower garden. It's open until two p.m.

"That sounds lovely," she said, looking forward to a stroll through the gardens.

"The chef make fabulous eggs benedict, so be sure to try them. Dinner is Thursday to Sunday, but reservations are recommended as it fills up fast. There's internet available in the media room, which is through that door," he said, pointing to the left of the huge living area that guests could share as they relaxed. "There's also a computer station on each of the two upstairs floors but no internet access on those. Jason Montpelier, the owner of the inn, prefers to keep the restoration of the place in keeping with the 1700's era when it was originally built."

The man was a wealth of information as he rattled off the information he knew by heart, having repeated it hundreds of times, she was sure. His love of his job showed in his attitude, making guests feel warm and welcome. "That's incredible. I can't wait to see my room." Angela slid the key into the front pouch of her purse and pulled her suitcase a little closer.

"If you decided to eat out, try Bixby's Diner. Katrina's cooking is amazing, and every morning she bakes fresh daily specials and donuts. Our chef is incredible, but if you like a change every now and then, Bixby's is the way to go. There's also Murphy's for Italian food, and Cade's Tavern offers other great choices for food and drink."

"For a small town, that's a lot of food." She shook her head and grinned.

Kyle nodded. "It is. Folks around here do like to eat."

The overhead bell chimed as another of the finalist walked in. Luckily, it wasn't

Justin. Time to move on if she didn't want a face-to-face meeting with the jerk anytime soon.

Angela climbed the stairs, lugging her suitcase with her. The door was wide open, but the number on the wall next to it showed she was in the right spot. She stepped inside and looked around. Kyle was right. The place looked as though she'd stepped back in time, the antique furniture and accessories reflecting a time period long gone. She loved the bedspread. Its patchwork design of roses and other flowers woven into squares had been meticulously stitched. The slightly yellowed and faded design showed its age and beauty like a faded flower, yet it was still clean.

The small lamp next to the bed had tiny roses adorning the base and appeared as though they were hand-painted. The antique furniture was hand crafted, each intricate scroll or design seemed to be made with loving care. She moved to close the door, peeking back into the hall to admire the painting on the wall.

A movement off to the left caught her attention as someone started up the stairs toward the third floor. The man glanced her way and stopped.

Grant Edwards. Angela frowned. What was he doing here?

He took a step backward and down, crossing the hall to approach. "Angela, it's lovely to see you again," his voice held a note of sincerity, but not one of surprise.

The question was, why? Because Angela was more than surprised—she was in shock. "What are you doing here, Grant?" she asked without preamble.

"The same thing you are, I would assume. The competition." He was a contestant. *No. No. No.* She had dinner with a competitor. When would she learn? She hadn't heard his name called. Although, she hadn't even heard her own name called after Justin's was announced. She'd been a fool. But then, Angela didn't remember seeing him on stage. Her evening of fun with Grant had come to a crashing halt, the memory of an enjoyable evening ruined.

Angela stiffened, not at all happy with the turn of events. "I see. I should be going. I still need to unpack, and dinner is at seven. We mustn't be late." A movement at the end of the hall caught her attention, her gaze landing on Justin outside the last door on the right. Apparently, she had used up all her good luck in the competition because having Grant and Justin here were two strokes of bad luck.

"We have plenty of time. Perhaps you would care to join me for a glass of wine in the bistro, or we could stroll through the gardens. I feel as though we need to talk—about the other night, that is."

Business discussions were taboo before, and now, more than ever, they were still taboo. His smile was disarming, but she forced herself not to succumb to his easy charm. "There's nothing to talk about—nothing happened. I refuse to mix business and pleasure and would prefer it if you did the same." Her chin rose a notch as she tried to take control of the situation.

Grant moved closer, his gaze intent on her. "I see. And I agree, except for one thing."

Angela couldn't resist asking, her curiosity kicking in a notch. "What's that?"

"We need to discuss last night. Since we're both here together and will be seeing more of each other."

"There's nothing to discuss. It was dinner. End of story."

"Not quite. I want to get to know everyone here, and that includes you. Especially you, as I'm intrigued—by your scent," he added with a grin.

It was just as she suspected. He was a finalist and the worst kind. The kind who wanted to weasel information out of you to see how they could use it to their advantage.

It was a pity because she had enjoyed her evening with him. "Well, you already know me, so cross me off your scheming list." She stood there, arms crossed and defensive.

The smile slid from his face, his brow drawn tight. "I'm sorry you feel that way." He turned to leave, paused, and then turned back as if to say something, before continuing up the stairs. Whatever it was, she was destined to never know.

Justin approached from the other direction. Another problem she'd have to deal with, but after her success with Grant, she was more than prepared. And there was still hope he didn't recognize her.

His gaze searched her face for mere seconds before he nodded. "Angela Bradbury, aka Lindsey Bradbury. I'm surprised to find you here." So much for Justin not recognizing her.

"Likewise. Although, surprised is a better word. You don't deserve to be here," Angela said, trying her best to sound disdainful while maintaining control. For years she'd thought of what she would say to him if she ever saw him again, but the words failed her.

"Ahhh, but I do. I've done quite well for myself as a perfumer for Contadine Fragrances. What's your story...oh, I remember—"

"That's enough, Justin. I won't listen to your lies." She turned to go into her room, refusing to have this discussion with him. It was like talking to a snake.

"Listen to this then because it's no lie. You're the one who doesn't belong here. And chatting up Grant Edwards isn't going to pave the way for you to win—he isn't the client. No one knows who that is, and he wouldn't be here at the Crestfield. You never were very smart, were you?" The vein in his temple had popped out, his anger not well hidden and reminding her of a gorilla.

The insults hurt, but four years had done a lot to help put everything in perspective and move forward to reestablish her reputation. If she made it through the next round, there was no reason she couldn't win the whole competition. Isabella's Honey Angel was her ace in the hole, and one no one else in the world could create. "Neither were you. One day, you'll pay for your lies. I know Grant isn't the client because he's one of the finalists. And if nothing else, you taught me not to trust anyone, so I won't be chatting him up. I leave the underhanded methods to you since you have loads of experience."

Justin laughed, shaking his head. "Don't expect me to believe you don't know he's the owner of Jaranda. I'm not that gullible." His laughter died, the expression on his face turning into a scowl. "Fair warning, don't go spreading any lies about me, or I'll make sure you get the raw end of the bargain," he snarled.

Grant Edwards. The name finally dropped into place and why she thought she recognized it. This was worse than a disaster. She'd had dinner with the owner of the company. No wonder he hadn't wanted to talk business, and no wonder he wasn't surprised to see her. "I think it's safe to say talking about you is the last thing I want to do. I think you do that very well yourself," she said, walking into her room and closing the door firmly before turning the lock. And all before Justin had a chance to answer.

There was trouble brewing at the inn, and Angela couldn't afford to make another mistake. Hopefully, Grant kept quiet about their dinner, or the others would wonder if there was something unethical going on. Justin's slimy brain was already thinking the worst, but it was something she too, had questioned. Was she a finalist because she'd had dinner with Grant, or did she make it on her own?

It was a question she wanted answered.

Chapter Five

CHLOE TURNED A HUGE smile on Captain Tremont, the excitement of new love on the horizon enough to turn her into a giddy but still ghostly mess. "Did you see what I saw?" she asked the handsome man next to her.

"I saw a woman who wants nothing to do with either of those men. She made it quite clear, my dear."

Men. He still didn't get it—not entirely anyway. It was time to enlighten him because this was clearly her new project. "You saw wrong. The tall, distinguished man is attracted to the woman, and her words didn't match her body language. You need to pay better attention to all the clues if you're going to get this matchmak-

ing business right." Chloe shook her head and laughed.

The captain had insisted on teaming up with her. Of course, that was after his honor as a naval officer had been restored, and he realized his love was for Chloe and not her twin sister, Claire. A wrong that had taken over two hundred years to right, but now the love of her life was by her side for eternity. An eternity she'd chosen to spend matchmaking likely people who simply needed a little extra push to see the truth right in front of their faces.

Captain Tremont had taken far too long to recognize the truth, something she didn't wish on the young couples who passed through the Crestfield Inn. Sometimes, people didn't get out of their own way long enough to see destiny staring them in the face.

"I'm sure you're right, my dear. You have a knack for knowing," he said, holding out his hand for hers.

Of course, she was right. When two people checked in and all the signs were there, including the chill of delight Chloe had come to recognize as it washed over her, that was when she and Captain Tremont stepped in to help. It didn't always work out that the couple went away happily-ever-after, but pretty darn close. It helped because she herself was in love and wanted everyone else to have the same happiness.

"Shall we go upstairs?" She placed her hand in his, and he led her back to the attic, where they spent most of their time dancing and talking, making up for the lost years.

"Yes, my dear. What do you propose we do to help them?" he asked as they floated up the stairs.

"I'm not sure yet, but it will come to me. You heard them. There's a dinner tonight, and I for one plan to be there." Hopefully, by then, an idea would come to her. Otherwise, she'd wing it.

"And I plan to accompany you, Miss Westerly."

"I was hoping you'd say that." Chloe laughed, falling into his arms for a dance.

"No, you knew I would say it," Captain Tremont said, the twinkle in his eyes a telltale sign he was teasing her.

Grant headed down the stairs, his gaze drifting towards the door that led to Angela's room. He'd half hoped they'd run into each other before dinner, the need to discuss a few things more than a little important. Once he'd caught sight of another of the contestants coming down the hall, he'd had no choice but to move up the stairs and out of sight.

The last thing he wanted was to make Angela uncomfortable, especially given it would seem she was already irritated with him. What he couldn't figure out was why. It's not like they hadn't agreed not to talk business, so why would he have mentioned who he was?

Hopefully, once she had time to think it over, she'd cool off a bit and see reason. Enough reason to spend time with him anyway—for the purposes of the competition, of course. "Hey, Kyle. Is everything set up for dinner this evening in the bistro?"

"Yes, sir. Just like you asked. We put together four tables and have twelve place settings laid out, with name tags on each setting. You said any order was fine, so I put them in alphabetical order. I like organization," Kyle said, chuckling.

The man touted he was the do-everything-guy around the place, and Grant had to agree. The owner had done well hiring him, Kyle's attitude and efficiency a huge plus for a customer-oriented business that would rely on excellent service and word-of-mouth advertising. "That will work. It's a formal way to be informal this evening. The next round is in two days, and I want everyone to relax, have a good time, and get to know one another. I want this to be a memorable experience for everyone, win or lose."

Kyle nodded. "I think tonight's dinner and tomorrow's agenda will do just that."

Grant hoped he was right. Just as he started to walk away, he suddenly remembered the maintenance issue he wanted to pass along. "By the way, there was a decent-sized draft coming from somewhere on the stairs between the second and third floor. You might want to have someone take a look. Hopefully, there isn't a leak to go along with it."

"So true. A house this old, it would destroy the integrity of the home. Thanks for telling me. I'll pass the information on to Mr. Montpelier."

Grant moved off, wanting to see for himself that all was in order in the restaurant. Kyle wasn't the only stickler for organization. He entered the bistro and glanced around, his gaze drawn to the name tags laid out at the top of each place setting. Starting at the head of the table, he walked around, noting each of the names, just as Kyle had mentioned. Angela was at the head of the table, her first name scoring her a prestigious seat. The problem with that, was it put Grant all the way at the other end.

The odds of ever seeing her again had been next to nil as the least experienced contestant in the group, and his joy came from knowing she'd beaten the odds and made it past the first round of cuts. She was quite a woman for sure—quite a perfumer, he added, trying to be politically correct.

But he was also honest enough to admit that the thought of spending the evening in her company for the second time gave him a sense of satisfaction. Grant wouldn't question his motives too closely; not sure he'd like what he found. The stirrings of attraction were where it started between two people, and then everything usually went downhill from there. Yes, some things were best left to fate, and his fate tonight was him sitting at the far end of the table.

Grant removed his coat and searched for his name tag, intent on putting his jacket on the back of the chair. Except his name tag was missing. He glanced at several of the others. They appeared in alphabetical order, but his was nowhere to be found where he would have expected it to be. He continued to make his way around the table and was surprised to find his tag next to Angela's.

Kyle's alphabet was a little off. He chuckled to himself, grabbed the tag, and headed for the correct spot, determined to fix the error. Reaching for the tag with William Bartlett's name on it where his tag should have been, he paused, glancing down at his own tag and then back at the now empty spot next to Angela.

It wasn't as if it was his mistake.

Grant shrugged before coming to a decision. He left William's tag where it was and moved to the place setting next to Angela. He put his own tag back to where he'd found it, just as some of the others began arriving at the bistro. Within minutes, more finalists and judges arrived, everyone locating their seats and striking up conversation with their dinner partners for the evening.

The low buzz in the room increased to a steady hum as voices grew louder. Grant knew the minute Angela walked into the room. She approached the table and found her spot.

"The head of the table. Nice," she said, pasting a smile on her face.

Grant could tell it was forced, and he wanted to put her at ease. She had no reason to be tense, and he much preferred she enjoy the experience. They would be wined and dined with the most selective and fascinating food choices the chef had chosen for the menu. The theme of course—aromatherapy of food. And Grant was more than interested in what she would think of each course, her poetic justice with words intriguing. "The name Angela is more than beautiful, it's also useful when life is alphabetized." He grinned, hoping to lighten the mood between them.

Her gaze flicked down to the place setting where he stood, a frown on her face. She reached over and picked up the tag, shaking her head. "Since when does a G even come close to an A with all these people in the room?" He knew what she was asking.

"I wouldn't know, but I opted not to correct someone's mistake."

"I see. So you're saying you didn't orchestrate this coincidental seating arrangement?" Her gaze held his steadfast and unyielding as she searched for the truth.

"No, why would you think that?" he asked, glad the mistake wasn't on him. He had a feeling she wouldn't have forgiven such a blatantly contrived set up for the two of them to spend dinner together. Not after she'd already made it clear she preferred to be on her own.

Angela glanced at some of the contestants who had taken a nearby seat and then leaned forward. "The same reason I wonder if you orchestrated today's outcome, Mr.

Edwards, *owner* of Jaranda—something you failed to mention," she asked, her voice low and tight.

"It was a mutual agreement not to discuss business the other evening, and you know it. And for the record, I had nothing to do with today's outcome. I'm not involved in the judging—merely here as an observer at this point. My company means a lot to me, and I wanted to meet the finalists and get to know them. If one of them is going to be working with the client, I need to make sure the client's interests are protected."

Angela nodded. "Okay, then. I believe you. But know this, I still won't talk business with you, no matter who you are. Deal?"

"Deal." He liked the fiery courage she had and her unwillingness to let anything get in the way of why she was here. It was the same single-minded determination he had when his grandfather taught him the business, and the same determination he was applying to the company now to make it a continued success.

"I told you I was right about those two," Chloe said, the glow of satisfaction welling up in her. Changing the name tags had been a genius idea, one she'd had to implement rather quickly. Luckily, Grant Edwards had been more intent on the overall room when he first arrived rather than the dancing cards at the table.

"You were, my dear. I never doubted you." Captain Tremont smiled down at her, love shining in his eyes.

"See that it stays that way. Can't afford another two hundred years to set the record straight." She laughed.

"Are you ever going to let me forget the error in my judgment."

"Not in this lifetime, mister. Captain or no captain, as the love of my life, I think I'm entitled."

"That you are, my dear. That you are," the captain said, nodding.

Chapter Six

DINNER HAD TURNED OUT to be a fun affair, despite Angela's misgivings when she arrived. Even Justin hadn't been able to dampen her spirits with the dark mood reflected on his face each time he glanced her way. She wasn't going to pay any attention to him. Between Anthony, Barbara, Ralph, and Grant, the conversation had stayed between them, almost as if the table were divided in two. It was awesome how they could all come together and relax, knowing what was at stake in round two of the competition.

The easy, relaxed attitude was something she envied. If it hadn't been for Justin, she might well be one of those people, but instead, she remained guarded. Luckily, she hadn't let her reservations control her ability to communicate or to enjoy the easy humor the others shared.

Although, dealing with Grant brought its own issues.

"Good night, everyone. What a wonderful dinner and I enjoyed getting to meet you all," Angela said, smiling at the others as she prepared to leave. Some were staying for another round of cocktails, but she wasn't one of them. Letting her inhibitions down with a second glass of wine wasn't on her agenda. Moderation had always been key and stood her in good stead.

"Good night," the others murmured.

"See you in the morning for our tour," Barbara added.

Angela was looking forward to the personal tour of the famous Bennington Gardens, her love of flowers pushing her out of her shell. Of course, between Grant and Barbara's insistence, the six people who'd made up her end of the table were arranged into the first group, leaving the others to form the second and later grouping. It worked well for Angela, considering that meant she wouldn't have to deal with Justin. "Yes. What a wonderful treat. I love flowers almost, or as much as perfume," she said, grinning.

"I'm going upstairs as well. I'll walk you to your door if you don't mind the company," Grant said, standing as if he knew she'd never say no.

"Of course. Telling the owner of Jaranda to go walk himself just wouldn't do," she teased, her comment eliciting laughter and nods from the others. It was a defense tactic that worked in her favor. The rest of the group would conclude she was doing what he asked because of who he was, not because it was by choice. It was best they thought it, even if it weren't entirely true. Either way, she would have said yes.

A dangerous answer, but one she would have given anyway.

"We'll all meet up here at 7:55. Breakfast starts at 6:30, so be sure to get plenty to eat. The chef here is from New York and makes a variety of spectacular dishes to whet your appetite. And his homemade jam is from a recipe handed down through the generations," Grant announced.

"Sounds good," Ralph said, lifting his hand in farewell. The others followed suit.

Angela led the way out of the bistro, Grant holding the door open for her. "That was fun," she said, smiling up at him. It was the only things she could think of saying.

"It was. I'm glad you're not mad at me anymore. I really enjoy your company and I'm pleased we'll be in the same group for the tour. And you can't blame me for orchestrating that, can you?" he asked, grinning down at her.

"True. But the jury's still out on the name tags," she added. In all honesty, she believed him, but it was better to keep him in the dark, hoping it would help keep things in line between them.

"I swear I didn't change them. I just didn't change them back when I noticed the mistake." Grant didn't look at all embarrassed by the admission, and it caused her heart to flutter.

Enough to tell him the truth and let him off the hook. "I believe you. Against my better judgment, but I do. And I also know you were right about the reason you didn't tell me about Jaranda. I was the one who said no business conversation first. I'm sorry if I accused you of dishonesty." Apologizing for being on edge and making a snap judgment, definitely new territory for her, mainly because she didn't make mistakes.

Not for the last four years anyway.

They arrived at her door, and she withdrew her key. "Thank you, and good night." Her words sounded inadequate, but she was at a loss as she fumbled to make the key work.

"Having trouble? Let me try," he said, reaching for the key. "I had trouble with mine earlier today also. Sometimes you have to jiggle it just right with these old keys." Grant winked, his chocolate brown eyes crinkling at the corners as he smiled. She could get lost in their depths if she wasn't careful.

"You must not be a good jiggler," she teased, as Grant struggled to unlock the door. "What should I do? Kyle has long since left the front desk, and I would hate to disturb Mr. Montpelier."

"Stay with me." Grant winked.

"You're incorrigible." Angela swatted at his shoulder playfully, but he managed to duck away before her hand connected.

"It was a joke. Given the circumstances, it wouldn't look good—for you."

"The circumstances?" She couldn't stop the question from slipping out.

"The competition," he said, his grin deepening.

Of course, the competition. She knew that, for the most part anyway. "And every other reasonable reason that goes with it. Like, I just met you two days ago. We live in different states. You're you, and I'm me. I have a job." She needed to shut up, each nervous reason she listed sounding more like she thought he was interested in a relationship.

"I wasn't offering you my bed, only my couch. I don't think the rest of your reasons have any bearing." Grant couldn't stop laughing.

She'd made a foolish mistake and crossed a line. Bad move at her own expense. "Well...in that case..." she drawled, determined to get one back at him, pausing as if she was reconsidering his offer.

His eyes grew wide, but he remained silent for the space of the few seconds she let the consideration hang between them.

"Ummm...no. Let me have my key." Angela held out her hand, unable to keep from smiling up at him.

Grant dropped it in the palm of her hand, his smile only a fraction of what it was once before.

Angela tried the lock again.

"I can call—"

"That won't be necessary," Angela said when the key turned on her first try this time. She pushed open the door. "I've got this from here, but thanks for your generous offer."

"Always a gentleman," he teased, appearing to have recovered.

"Let's hope so. See you in the morning." Angela closed the door and leaned against it. There could never be anything between them, for all the reasons she'd given. Deep down, Angela still wanted love, marriage, and a family...she just wasn't sure it was God's plan for her life.

Chloe watched as Grant moved up the stairs. The dinner had gone remarkably well this evening, but her limited abilities weren't much good when it came to jamming the lock. She would have to do better next time. The two clearly had sparks between them, and the energy was undeniable—but the competition was a problem. She would have to think of a way to overcome the barrier, but for now, she needed to hurry—Captain Tremont had promised her a dance.

The following morning, Grant headed for the bistro in need of a strong cup of coffee. He hadn't slept well at all, which was unusual for him. The problem was a case of Angela on the brain.

With each toss and turn, he swore he could smell her perfume. Not that he had any intentions of telling Angela that he couldn't get her fragrance out of his head—or her, for that matter.

Grant entered the bistro, pleased to see most of the others already there. His gaze darkened when he spotted Angela and Justin in the far corner of the room, the two deep in conversation. Grant wasn't jealous. At least that's what he tried to convince himself with each glance in their direction.

He was tempted to join them, curious about what they would need to discuss with such a degree of privacy, when as far as he knew, they were strangers. Angela hadn't spoken to the man at all last evening. Grant started in their direction as Barbara grabbed his arm.

"Everyone's here and ready to go. This will be so much fun," she said, not bothering to drop her hand off his arm.

"I think so, too. Angela's over there; I'll go get her, and then we can head out on the first shuttle."

"No, I'll let her know we're leaving. I wanted to say goodbye to Justin. We got to know each other over cocktails last night. Charmer for sure. Not to mention curious, but nice." Barbara laughed and sauntered off in their direction, leaving him no choice but to take the lead and prepare the group for departure.

Within ten minutes, the first group were loaded on the shuttle bus, and they were almost ready to roll.

"Good morning again, everyone," Grant said over the microphone once they were all situated. As you know, I've arranged a tour of the Bennington Gardens, which isn't far from here. They have a combination of garden arrangements sure to catch the interests of any dedicated perfumer. Walking through the gardens will help clear the mind, allowing you to search for the fragrance that appeals to your soul, the one you can create with all your heart. Aside from that, they're beautiful," he added, laughing.

The group joined in the laughter, everyone primed for a trip that would excite their senses—a perfumer's dream venture.

"We've split our group up into two groups of six, as that's the most people the owner allows in any building or garden at a time. He feels more than that is distracting and overpowering, and I tend to agree. So, relax, enjoy the ride and the tour, and afterward, there is a basket lunch with your name on it being served in the arboretum—compliments of Chef James from the Crestfield Inn. Another lesson in culinary delights, I'm sure. The other's will be joining us for lunch and then continue on with their tour. This afternoon and tonight, you're on your own to explore and venture out before round two tomorrow."

Grant took a seat in front of Angela and Barbara. Angela hadn't said a word to him yet, and by the looks of things, she was tense, leaving him to wonder what was wrong. It was too early to be upset with him, unless of course, it had carried over from last night. Although, he didn't think she'd be one to hold grudges.

Justin. He didn't understand what the problem would be, but he felt sure Angela wasn't likely to answer even if he asked. He turned in his seat to face them. "Good morning, Angela. I haven't had a chance to speak with you yet. Did you sleep well?"

"Good morning. And yes, I did. Surprisingly. Flowers are a passion of mine, so my excitement last night was like a teenage girl going to prom." She smiled, but it wasn't quite the same natural, easy smile he had come to know. Something was off.

"I'm glad you approve. I wanted to find something to get everyone out from the inn so they could enjoy the area and take home more memories than just the competition." There could only be one winner, and it was important to him that everyone saw it as a positive experience. He knew all too well how consuming this business could be.

"Well, you're certainly doing that." Her smile brightened ever so slightly, which was a good sign—for him. At least he wasn't the object of her displeasure.

Barbara reached out to touch his arm as though to get his undivided attention. "I once went to the Villa Carlotta gardens in Italy, and they were incredible. It took two whole days to see everything because I took time to stop and smell the roses."

Grant inwardly cringed at the cliché. She was a perfumer and should have been able to describe her experience much more eloquently. Cliché was not what he was looking for should she make it through to round three.

"What about you, Angela? Any favorite gardens?" he asked, trying to draw her into the conversation.

She nodded, a shuttered look crossing her face. Not exactly the reaction he'd been looking for. "It's called Izzy's. I'm sure you've never heard of it." Angela shrugged. "Just a small place, but one I love to visit for the simple pleasure of thinking and letting my imagination visualize and create exquisite fragrance combinations," she said, her voice taking on a wistful tone.

Her answer was evasive, making him more than a little curious. "I'm not familiar with that one. Where is it located? Perhaps I should check the place out sometime."

Angela's eyes widened into round saucers, her head shaking an answer before the words rolled out. "Not far from where I live. It's just an old woman's private garden. I doubt she or her granddaughter would appreciate you showing up."

The comment was a clear end of the discussion and a firm dismissal of his suggestion. Barbara carried most of the conversation for the duration of the ride to the gardens.

The owner met up with the group, giving them a brief history of the place and the concept behind the layout and the various sections. He led them through the first building, explaining the design and purpose, pointing out some of the most recent blossoms, their striking beauty as they opened vibrant with aroma and color.

On several occasions, Grant found himself next to Angela, the two of them examining the same flowers. "I like this one," he said, pointing to an orange and white orchid. "The petals are flawless, and the bouquet lingers in the air. It's like a mid-summer dream."

"They're lovely and have an almost ethereal quality with their delicate softness, yet vibrant and striking against the green foliage." She spoke in hushed tones, preserving the sanctity of the garden atmosphere.

"The orchid reminds me of you in a way. Intriguing," he said, gazing down at her. He'd left out the part that the orange dancing in the petals reminded him of her perfume. Something he hadn't been able to get out of his head since meeting her.

Given that she'd made it this far in the competition, Grant had to wonder if the fragrance was her own. She was certainly capable, and clearly, he'd underestimated her experience. To be in the top eight in this competition carried with it a certain degree of finesse and finely tuned skills. It was hard to imagine her skills came from a relative as listed on her application.

"Nothing intriguing about me." She laughed, her cheeks tinged with pink.

"I'll have to take your word on it, which would put us back to even. Now that we've learned to trust each other, I wanted to ask you something. I noticed you talking to Justin this morning, and you didn't seem at ease. I hadn't realized you two knew each other. Is everything okay?"

"We were just talking, and everything's fine. Thanks for asking," she said, moving off to the next display of orchids. "Look at this. It's lovely."

"It is." Grant wasn't looking at the orchid, as it was Angela who held his interest. Her answer was no more than he expected, but it did manage to raise his curiosity a notch or two. It was something that bore watching, considering what was at stake. If Justin was bothering her, he wanted to know. The guy had a good reputation as a perfumer, not to mention, the skill level to make it this far, but Grant had yet to figure out if he liked the guy.

And not just because of Angela. Or at least he hoped not.

There wasn't much opportunity to ask Angela any more questions for the rest of the tour. Whether by design or coincidence, she was always with the others in their group. Between all six of them, there was an easy camaraderie. He found it interesting that Angela's opinions mirrored his own, and he admired the eloquence with which she described the blossoms and their fragrance.

It was the same eloquence in her writing that won her the spot in the final fifty.

Chapter Seven

IT WAS EARLY DAWN, the light of the sky slowly driving out the shadows of the room. Angela stretched, rolled out of bed, and donned her robe. Today was another big day, and she needed to focus. Which meant no more thinking of Grant Edwards or the dinner date he'd been on last night.

How was she to know when he'd asked her to dinner, that there were two other finalists issued the same invitation? Angela had already declined the offer, thinking it would have been far too intimate and date-like. Changing her decision after the fact would have looked odd, not to mention, revealing her excuse as a lie. She could kick herself for saying no in the first place—when what she had really wanted to do was say yes.

His comments about the orchid and comparing it to her had taken Angela off guard. The woman in her couldn't help but be pleased with the compliment. She'd been on edge after another sour and disconcerting conversation with Justin, and then Grant's question about her own favorite garden pushed her warning and proceed-with-caution buttons to a high level she couldn't ignore. It was her grandmother's garden, the place where Isabella had first started cultivating roses, and it was where Angela had produced *Isabella's Honey Angel.*

It was the place Angela still worked on her creations, even though her heart still ached for her grandmother, wishing she was by her side to help guide her along the way. Although, she was grateful her grandmother hadn't seen Angela's fall from grace in the perfuming world. Isabella would have charged to her rescue and demanded satisfaction for the truth. Four years later, Angela would do the same. She wasn't the young, naïve girl she had been back then.

But this competition was everything to her, and with Justin in the mix, she had to be careful. Her only hope going forward was to stay away from him, steer clear of Grant, and let fate take its course. With any luck, Justin wouldn't move to the finals.

Right on time, she arrived at Liberty Park. Only eight tents stood in a row this time, each with a coordinator guarding who went in and out. The judges were wandering around and talking to people, and she spotted Grant near the stage just as he climbed the stairs and stepped up to the microphone.

"Good morning, everyone," he said, his voice bright, cheery, and welcoming.

Everyone murmured good morning in response and then quickly fell silent, eager to hear what was next.

"Today is the second elimination round. Congratulations to you all for making it this far. As before, you each have a tent and a coordinator, and your tables are preset and locked. The difference, however, is that you will have twenty-five essential oils and your time allocation limited to one hour. Limited resources and time force you to rely on instinct and allows us to see how natural the perfuming process comes to you. The judges will collect the eight samples and then, shortly before lunch, report back to us with the results." Dressed in a suitcoat and tie, Grant looked exceedingly handsome as he made his announcement. He was a man used to being in control, confidence vibrating on every word. "Any questions?"

"Can you tell us more about the final round and how it will work if we make it?" David asked.

Thank you, Angela mouthed under her breath, wondering the same thing.

"I can. The client, who wishes to remain confidential, will accept the previously formulated samples from the three finalists chosen today. He will forward his final decision to me, and I will announce the winner of the twenty-five thousand dollars and the contract to work with the client to produce a signature-line fragrance." Angela's heart raced at the possibilities a win would bring. She needed this to prove to herself and her grandmother, she could do it and that all her grandmother's efforts to train her hadn't been in vain.

"Thank you. Any idea of a time frame for the final results?" Heather asked.

"Why? You in a hurry to leave?" Grant teased.

"No, just on edge. Sorry," Heather said, her cheeks flushed red.

"Don't apologize; it's okay to be curious. I think his plans are to select the winner as early as tomorrow, so you won't have long to wait."

Tomorrow this could all be over. Angela had never been this nervous—not even four years ago when her world had fallen apart before she even realized what was happening.

No one else spoke.

"Please check in to get your assigned tent number. Good luck, everyone." Grant moved off the stage, stopping to talk to one of the judges.

Angela headed for the registration table to get her number. There were no rule packets to hand out this time since the format was the same. At the designated moment, they would all know what today's creation assignment would be. Angela hoped it was something she could identify with, knowing how important it was to think, feel, and smell the right ingredients.

Twenty minutes later, the coordinator unlocked her desk and removed the cover, revealing the twenty-five essential oils she would work with. Angela picked up the envelope and clutched it to her chest.

"Good luck," the woman said, a gentle, reassuring smile on her face. They all knew how important this round was to each entrant. The chance for a signature fragrance was as daunting as euphoric sensations came.

"Thank you," she said, opening the envelope. Angela preferred to rely on prayers over luck but wouldn't say no to the extra well wishes. Adrenaline rushed through her, and she took a few deep breaths, trying to calm her emotions as she read the words.

Free for all.

Limited oil. Limited time. Unlimited possibilities.

This was her specialty. Angela nodded, knowing she could do this. Whether she made the cut or not remained to be seen, but she would turn in something fantastic. One by one, she noted the oils, mentally picturing what they represented and drawing strength from the ones that spoke the loudest to her. Not in concentration, but in subtle, soft power that evoked emotions. Perfumes reflected the heart and soul, and the trick was deciding what she wanted it to show.

Intriguing. It was the word Grant had used to describe Angela. The truth was she found him intriguing. Reflecting on what she knew about Grant, she tried to zero in on the essence of that feeling, using him as her inspiration. She started to mix and create a fragrance that was soft yet lingering, undeniable. Using only a handful of oils, she mixed them together, listening to an inner sense of how much was just enough.

Her grandmother once said, too much is when your brain starts to question whether to add more or not. Angela chose orange for her top notes simply because it was her favorite. Drop by drop, she added the middle notes, sticking with rose and lemongrass, positive the lemon as a tail to the orange would keep one guessing, while the rose would lure one in softly, enticing them to know more as they tried to identify the source. For the base notes, the ones that would last with someone the longest and therefore stick with the judges, she used jasmine, patchouli, and cedarwood. They were strong yet sensual and addictive scents, and yet in a soft and pleasing way.

She stopped mixing, sensing she'd reached that moment—and with ten minutes to spare. Smiling, she took one last gentle sniff, deemed it perfection, and capped the bottle, not wanting to diminish the early tones of the fragrance in any way. The judges needed the whole experience.

"I'm done," Angela called out.

"Wow, nicely done and with such confidence." The woman tagged her sample, letting Angela sign off on it like she'd done before.

"Thank you. I think I'll take a walk if that's okay. I want to clear my head."

The woman nodded, the two of them walking toward the entrance. “You have some time before they start serving lunch.”

“Who can eat at a time like this?” Angela asked. Even though she was done working on her submission, her nerves hadn’t calmed one iota.

“I was wondering the same thing,” the woman said, chuckling. “I’d be a bag of jumping beans inside.”

“That describes the feeling perfectly.” Angela laughed. She stepped out of the tent, letting the sun beat down on her face.

“Already done?” Grant asked, startling her.

“I am. I feel good about this.” She smiled, unable to resist sharing what she considered a favorable outcome from the assignment.

“That’s great. Perhaps we could go to dinner and celebrate? I’m still holding out for more get-to-know-you time.” He winked.

“You did say you have nothing to do with the decisions, right?”

"The judges make the decisions for today and the client makes the decision for the final selection."

"We don't know anything yet, but I'll consider it if I make the cut. Otherwise, I'll be leaving right away. How's that for an answer?"

"I like a maybe." Grant chuckled. He looked at her as if wanting to add something. It was an intense look that made her heart skip a beat. He leaned forward, and she had the strangest feeling he was about to kiss her.

"Grant," she squeaked.

His arms came around her and pulled her close, his mouth going toward the side of her face, his lips landing on her cheek. "Good luck," he said.

Either he was a terrible aim, or he'd changed his mind. The words good luck pushed her to believe it meant he'd changed his mind, or she'd misread his expression altogether. It was better this way, but it didn't stop the telltale tug in her chest that felt like disappointment.

Several others headed their way, and the time for introspection would have to wait.

Chapter Eight

GRANT HAD ALMOST MADE a huge mistake. Kissing Angela might have been a spontaneous desire lodged deep in his brain that escaped, but luckily, he'd come to his senses before the damage was done.

The hug, on the other hand, brought him in close enough to inhale the fragrance Angela wore. *Rose d' Orange*. The name of the familiar scent popped into his head; the mystery fragrance identity finally solved. It was one that had come out years ago and had been quite successful initially but then faded out just as quickly. It didn't have the lingering power that most women looked for, but it also fell flat on the soft notes.

He'd liked it, but they were the same reasons it hadn't become a favorite of his. But on Angela, it was incredible. She must have bought multiple bottles back when it was on the market, which made it more interesting that she hadn't remembered the name. Even more so because she wore it every day. Maybe it meant nothing, but a sixth sense had him thinking about it more than he cared to.

If she came to dinner with him, he'd be sure to ask her more questions. He'd told the truth; today's results would be decided by the judges, and he had zero input. If she made it through this round, it was on her own. Grant hated the need to hedge a bit on his answer on the final decision. A little white lie, his mother once called them.

A lie was a lie. But there was no way he could reveal he was the client. Besides, the samples of the finalists would be anonymously marked, so it's not like he'd know which one was hers *if* she made it.

Liar. The more time he spent with Angela, the more he understood her. And based on her personality and aura alone, he'd know which scent she created. There was a magical air about her that was undeniable.

Grant prided himself on fairness, and he would stand strong on that score. The person who designed the new signature fragrance would rise to instant fame within the company and be known worldwide, representing Jaranda. It had to be someone selected not only for their skill, but also their personality as they would be the new face of the company. It's why he insisted on getting to know the contestants.

His gaze frequently drifted to Angela. He would have liked to remain by her side, offering words of support, but he didn't want any hint of impropriety connected to her name before the judges decided.

"Have you decided?" Grant asked the judges as they approached.

"We did. It wasn't easy, but the three we picked were the top scoring. One still continues to surprise us, but as you know, we don't see the names until after we've finalized our scores," Anthony, the lead judge stated, the others nodding in agreement.

"That's all that matters." Dare he hope they meant Angela? It had surprised him she made it this far and little surprised him. Her experience and abilities weren't matching up, but she was the real deal. "Shall we do this? I think the contestants are getting antsy, and by the looks of things, they aren't hungry."

"More likely afraid to throw it up from the stress," Lacy said, leading the group toward the stage.

"I'm sure you're right." Grant chuckled. "Ladies and gentlemen, if I could have your attention, please." Those that hadn't noticed them approach the stage immediately moved forward to join those who had. The group of contestants huddled close, each one a hopeful expression on their face.

•♥•♥•♥•♥•♥•

The biggest moment of Angela's life was upon her, and she closed her eyes. *Please, Lord, give me the strength to hold my head up high, no matter what happens.* She knew that becoming one of the final three would open doors in the perfuming industry, helping to put the past behind her. Winning the contest would be amazing and the easiest route, but Angela understood the tough competition she was up against. She had to remain grounded about her chances of winning and being able to open her own business.

"Good afternoon, everyone," Grant called out.

Angela opened her eyes and looked around one last time. Everyone here was hopeful they'd be selected, but only three would have the chance of a lifetime.

"The judges have said this was unbelievably close. Excellent job, everyone. Putting a fast time limit on your creation was designed to show your intuitive side, the soul of perfuming. As a reminder to those who make it to the final round, your sample is due in with the judges by eight a.m. tomorrow morning. Best of luck to all of you. In no particular order, the first of the three finalists who will get to submit their own personal creation is David Reese."

"Yes," David exclaimed. Those around him clapped him on the back, congratulating him.

"Come up here on stage. We'll want a photo of the finalists," Grant said, pointing toward where the judges stood. He opened the second envelope. "The second finalist is Justin Lockwood." *Not again.*

"Woohoo," Justin cried out, accepting the congratulations of the others.

Angela had no choice but to follow suit. "Congratulations, Justin," she said, the words bitter in her mouth.

He shot her a quick look of surprise and then smirked. "The best always wins," he said in a low voice before turning away and jumping up on the stage.

"Once a jerk, always a jerk," she mumbled. Angela instantly regretted responding, letting him get to her. If Justin was right, he wouldn't win. A liar and a cheat could never be the best—but then, look how far he'd made it. He must have learned something along the way. Of course, he did. Justin got to attend the perfume school in her place after his false accusation got her fired.

Angela drew in a deep breath as Grant opened the third and final envelope.

"The last finalist is—Angela Bradbury."

Her eyes filled with tears. He said her name. He really said her name. Angela Bradbury. *Thank you, Lord.* She wanted to pinch herself to believe it was real. The others started to hug her, some kissing her cheek. They were genuinely happy for her, even if it meant the end of their hopes. She'd met such great people during the past few days, and they'd made the entire experience special. *All except Justin*. But she didn't want to think about him right at this moment.

"Get up on stage, honey," Barbara said, giving her a shove.

Angela shook her head and laughed. "I'm going." She passed Grant, who stood smiling, a gentle nod of his head making her feel warm and special. Moving to stand next to David, she didn't dare look at Justin, certain he'd ruin her good mood.

"Thank you everyone for entering, and from my heart and Jaranda's, we wish you the absolute best in the future. To have made it this far, you are all quite exceptional artisan perfumers," Grant said, another round of applause bursting from the ones who hadn't made it.

She knew they were heartbroken, and yet they clapped anyway, showing their true character.

Grant moved to shake hands with each of the finalists. "Congratulations," he said, squeezing Angela's hand a little tighter.

"Thank you." Angela grinned, finally acknowledging the truth. She'd made it to the final round. *Isabella's Honey Angel* would get its chance to entice the client—*and win twenty-five thousand dollars.*

The photographer took several photos with Grant and the judges. "Can we get one of just the finalists?" the man asked. "Let's put Angela in the middle. It's more balanced that way."

Angela cringed. It's not like she had a choice. David moved to her other side. Angela was unwilling to move, forcing Justin to be the one to move closer. He was all smiles and charm for the camera, but she knew he'd be angry she was still in the running.

She glared at him when he put his arm around her shoulder, but when David did the same, she choked down the retort that came to her lips. *Lord, get me through this with dignity and grace.* Pasting on a smile, she looked up at the camera.

"That's it, thank you," the man said moments later.

Angela stepped away, reviled by Justin's touch. She crossed the stage, prepared to leave, surprised when someone took her arm to help her down the steps. Looking up, she yanked her arm back when she realized it was Justin.

"Don't think you made it because of any great skill you possess. I'm sure you've bedazzled Grant Edwards, the same way you tried it with me. He'll get your number the same way I did."

"Your memory is sadly lacking, almost as much as your perfuming skills four years ago," she snapped.

“My memory is fine. It’s you that seems to have forgotten my earlier warning. Best of luck, Angela.” Justin turned and walked away.

In his arrogance, he hadn’t even realized the greater insult was to his perfuming skills. But the reminder of his warning worried her. The one thing she knew for sure, was that Justin Lockwood was capable of anything.

Chapter Nine

GRANT HAD COMPLETELY FORGOTTEN he'd promised to take the judges out to dinner that evening. They had done a splendid job, and it was important for him to honor their commitment to the cause.

He'd looked around for Angela to make his apologies, but she was nowhere in sight. It wasn't as though she'd agreed to have dinner with him yet, but it would have been good to let her know he couldn't make it anyway. Grant figured she left right after the photos were taken. Knowing her, she was back in her room making sure her sample was perfect. When it came to Angela's dedication and commitment to succeed, there was no question of her passion or her work ethic.

It was for the best they didn't have dinner, at least until the competition was over. And then, she'd be gone anyway. There was no sense in letting the friendship between them grow stronger, or the attraction for that matter. Because for the first time in a long time, Grant would have considered going on an official date—with Angela.

Getting caught up in discussions, it was a good two hours later by the time he made his way back to the Crestfield Inn. "Good evening, Kyle. Any messages?"

The young man glanced at the computer screen and then turned to do a quick check of the individual boxes on the wall. "None. Exciting day. Three happy contestants returned, two of them already having left to go celebrate. Most of the others have already packed and left or made arrangements to head home."

"It's always toughest on those that don't make it. The judges had difficult decisions to make. My understanding is that the quality of creativity was quite high." Grant ran a hand through his hair and then massaged the muscles of his neck briefly, stretching from side to side. It had been a long day, and he still had dinner to get through.

"So now what?" Kyle asked. "I mean, like what's the process for the three still in the running?"

"They turn in a sample of their own personally created fragrance to the judges by eight a.m. tomorrow. They had months to perfect the perfume to be used for this part of the contest if they made it to the finals. The samples will be delivered to the client, and he'll have twenty-four hours to decide a winner and will then let me know. At that point, I will make the official announcement."

"So, what's with the big secrecy of the client? Is he someone famous?"

Grant smiled. "I don't know. Perhaps he didn't want the publicity or speculation that would go along with an event this size. It was his request for total confidentiality, so we've honored it."

"I think it's kind of cool. Mysterious sort of." Kyle laughed. "It sure has people around town trying to guess who it might be."

Grant shrugged. Luckily, they wouldn't guess him, which is another reason he thought it important to make an appearance. "If you say so. Is Angela Bradbury in? I needed to speak with her?" He wanted to set the record straight for the night, just in case she did decide to give in to his dinner request.

Kyle nodded. "I think so. I've had to run a few errands around the inn, but I hadn't seen her leave while I was tending the front desk."

"Okay, thanks." Grant headed up the staircase, stopping on the second landing outside her door.

Knock. Knock. He waited a few moments, but she didn't answer.

Knock. Knock. Either she wasn't answering, or Kyle had missed her departure. Either way, the result was the same—there was no opportunity to tell her about his change in plans. Grant headed up the next flight of stairs to the third floor and his room. Glancing at his watch, he knew he had to hustle as there were only fifteen minutes to spare until he had to meet the judges for dinner.

He changed his shirt and tie and donned a suit coat for the occasion. After splashing on a bit of cologne he headed for the door and down the two flights of steps. Grant stopped at the front desk. "Hey, Kyle. Angela didn't answer her door. Can you give her a message for me?"

"Sure thing," Kyle said, handing him a pen and paper. "Write it down, and I'll put it in her room mailbox."

Angela,

Sorry. Forgot I had dinner plans with the judges. Perhaps tomorrow night? I'd like to talk to you about something.

Grant

Somewhere between the crazy idea to ask her to dinner and the crazy realization it would be a mistake judging by how much he was coming to care for her, another even crazier idea hit him. Maybe it was that he couldn't get her out of his head for a completely different reason than that of her fragrance lingering on his brain. Maybe this was love. A different kind of love than he'd shared with Amanda. This was more of a heaven-sent love, and the peace that came with it, a far deeper and satisfying emotion than what he'd experienced in the past. No matter what the results of the competition, Grant didn't want Angela walking out of his life.

And the way to make that happen was to have her come to work at Jaranda. Her instinctive talents would be better utilized as a member of his team, and it wasn't as if he were stealing her away from another perfumery. The bonus, of course, would be the ability to have more time to get to know Angela better without any commitment. A safe way to allow him time to sort out his feelings and discover if God was showing him a new direction he hadn't planned for in his life.

Grant handed the message to Kyle.

"Oh yeah, I almost forgot. You've got a message. It was dropped off not long ago by a courier," Kyle said, handing him an envelope.

Glancing down, Grant noticed there was nothing to identify the sender. Angela? Which didn't seem likely since it was a courier. He slid his finger under the seal to open the letter, his curiosity peaked.

A strong fragrance assailed him seconds before Grace moved to stand next to him, her hand on his arm. "Hey, Grant. I'm looking forward to dinner this evening. With all the judging duties keeping me busy, we haven't had a chance to talk much. Buy me a drink, and we can chat before the others arrive," she said, her bright red lips forming a smile.

"Sounds like a plan." Grant stuffed the envelope in the breast pocket of his coat. His curiosity would have to wait—duty called.

###

Three hours later, Grant closed the door behind him, relieved for the peace and quiet. Between business conversation and friendly banter, not to mention a few of the remaining contestants joining them, it had been a non-stop night. In hindsight, he should have held the dinner at a different location. Angela hadn't been one of the ones to join them, leaving him to wonder where she'd gone.

Grant hung up his coat and headed for the bedroom to change into jeans and a t-shirt. The face of Jaranda wasn't afforded such luxury as comfort in clothing, the dress code ingrained in him at an early age. But how he dressed in the privacy of his own rooms was his choice.

He returned to the main area and poured a glass of wine, wanting to unwind from a busy day. Sitting on the sofa, he noticed his suitcoat on the floor. He crossed the room to pick up the jacket, knowing the dry-cleaning nightmare it would be if it wrinkled, or worse, picked up a stain. Reaching down to retrieve it, he spotted the envelope Kyle had given him earlier.

Grant pulled it from the breast pocket and hung up the coat, making sure it was hung correctly this time. He returned to the couch, slid open the envelope, and pulled out the card.

Sometimes appearances are not what they seem. You have a finalist by the name of Angela Bradbury who comes with a past marked with a caution flag. Check her background or look the fool if she wins. Trust me, as one almost duped by her, consider yourself forewarned.

Grant's heart about stopped when he read Angela's name in connection to the warning. Earlier, he had wondered if something was amiss with her disappearance but had shoved aside the doubt. He flipped the card over. *No signature.*

His stomach clenched. This could be a hoax by a jealous contestant who didn't make it to the finals. But Grant knew in his heart that he couldn't ignore the warning, especially given Angela's lack of official training or schooling.

Grant let out a deep breath. He needed answers, and he needed them fast. Tomorrow was just around the midnight corner, and after that, the twenty-four-hour timer started once the samples were turned in. Typing out a message to Alan, he could only hope his vice-president could work magic and get him the answers needed.

As he lay in bed, thoughts plagued him long into the night. Had Angela been playing him all along? Had she thought he had pull with the judging? Or with the client? The last thought hit hard, sounding far too logical and more like the truth.

As the owner of the Jaranda, Grant had full knowledge of the client's identity—something everyone else would realize as well.

Chapter Ten

ANGELA STILL COULDN'T BELIEVE she'd finaled. After rushing back to her room, she'd hidden out, not even bothering to answer the insistent knock at her door last night. She hadn't promised Grant a dinner date, and after much thought, knew it was best if she stayed away from him. She trusted no one, and with Justin's renewed warning, she felt it best to avoid any chance run-ins.

Her stomach was in knots, worrying about what he would do. He couldn't steal her formula this time, as the samples were already prepared, and Angela hadn't told a soul about her creation. Nor would she unless she won, and then, only to the client under a confidentiality contract.

Her grandmother was the one who came up with the idea of cultivating their own roses to create a unique fragrance. Angela had intensified the efforts to grow a rose more fragrant and captivating, something unique and lasting in its molecular makeup. The result was *Isabella's Honey Angel*, a blossom that opened in the evening, peaking at midnight in its floral intensity. And each year, she did trial after trial, mixing various oils with the oil from the rose, praying instincts would tell her when it was right.

The contest had been perfect timing with the sample she'd created, which took eight weeks to bring out the lingering floral notes. She hadn't been able to resist her favorite addition of orange essence, the citrusy touch giving life to the delicate yet sustainable rose fragrance.

Angela couldn't resist dabbing on a little of the new perfume. It was like rewarding herself for making it this far in the competition. A hint of daring to add to the excitement. Besides, other than dropping off the sample to Grace, Angela intended to stay in her room. *Away from any chance run-in with Justin.*

It was all or none at this point, and wearing the new scent changed nothing for the three finalists. It was a first, to wear it out in public. She dabbed it on her wrists and behind her ears, just a touch. The sweet, delicate fragrance clung to her like a second skin, enveloping her in a peaceful warmth. Perfection. She locked her personal sample back in the lockbox and hid it in the closest, taking the contest entry vial and placing it in a small box, and then in her purse. One couldn't be too careful with the contents.

At ten minutes until the deadline, Angela took a deep breath and headed downstairs to meet Grace. From there, Grace would deliver the samples to Grant, who would then deliver them to the client. And then it would be a waiting game.

The most nerve racking twenty-four hours in her life.

Angela couldn't help but wonder who the client was, but his brief had been enticing enough for her to move out of the shadows and into the limelight. As she rounded the bend at the bottom of the stairs, she was surprised to see Grace in deep conversation with Grant.

Perhaps he'd come to wish her good luck, the thought intriguing. They looked up as she approached, but it was Grant she focused on, the scowl on his face not at all what she expected. Was he upset because she hadn't gone to dinner with him? She had never agreed, so being angry would be a bit of an overreaction—and not at all like the man she'd come to know.

"Good morning." Angela smiled at Grace, preferring to ignore Grant and his ominous scowl. "Here's my sample," she said, holding the little box that held the vial out to her.

Grace took the box, returning the smile. "Good morning, dear. Right on time. I like it."

"I need to have a word with Angela. Could you excuse us, please, Grace?" Grant cut in with not so much as an ounce of a smile or pleasant exchange.

A sense of dread filled Angela., A sense of déjà vu hit her hard—the feeling one she remembered from four years ago.

Grace looked back and forth between them, her brow furrowed. "Sure. I'll just take the sample to my room and lock it up with the others, now that I have all three." She hesitated only a moment before heading up the stairs, leaving Angela alone with Grant.

"What's wrong?" Angela asked, needing to know the worst. Except, instinctively, she knew—maybe not the what, but certainly the who.

Justin Lockwood.

"I received a message last night with a tip about your past in this business. I was loathed to give it any credence and had my VP check into the claim and research your background more thoroughly. The report I received this morning came as quite a shock, although I'm sure you know what it said." Lines of tension marred his forehead, his angry scowl proof he believed everything he'd read.

"Of course, I do. But none of it's true—"

"The company who fired you says otherwise, and for someone with zero experience and training at the time, it's more than plausible. But that's in the past, and this is now."

Now? As in maybe he hadn't believed the story, or maybe he didn't care. Angela started to hope she would still have a chance, that Justin hadn't destroyed her reputation again. "Thank—"

"Don't, Angela. I've thought about this long and hard. You changed your name to avoid detection, which shows me you're still dishonest. Honesty is an integral part of someone's character, and I must inform you that you've been disqualified from the competition." His voice had grown cold as he delivered the news.

Shock vibrated through Angela, her stomach clenching with a violence that threatened to toss out her morning breakfast. Grant's demeanor had gone from yesterday's charm to today's dream-smashing taskmaster. "Disqualified? So it doesn't matter that I got here on my own? You simply believe the past and ignore everything I've done to bring the best I could to this competition? I'm in the finals because of my abilities. Surely you don't intend to discount my skills because of the past." *It wasn't fair*. It hadn't been then, and it wasn't now. The last time she hadn't fought back, but this time, she wouldn't walk away without speaking her mind.

Grant nodded. “I do. It’s about character. If you’d used your real name and not tried to pull the wool over my eyes, it might have been a different outcome.”

Easy for him to say now. “Might? There’s a non-committal word if I ever heard one. And just for the record, if I’d used my real name, I wouldn’t have gotten into the competition in the first place.”

“I guess we’ll never know. I’m sorry, Angela. You’re out, and I think it best if you leave the inn before the news breaks. It will be easier for you to fade into the background, and I’ll deal with the fallout and the press. Perhaps you should lay low a few days.” His eyes softened as he let out a deep breath.

“Easier for you maybe, while you’ve just ripped away my dreams. I thought you were above the typical kind of person who only looked on the surface. Shows you how wrong I was about you. Willing to condemn and judge based on a newspaper story. Did you even try to dig deeper? Don't you find it interesting there's no mention of actual charges ever being filed? No proof, no charges. And if you had looked even harder, you would have found out I was never asked my side of the story. It was a case of a perfumer versus a lowly sales employee. Of course, the accusations were never anything but believable. No one cared about the truth. And you're just like all the rest."

Grant shook his head, a dark expression on his face. He turned and walked away, leaving her standing there without even the smallest courtesy of a response.

Angela ran up the stairs, needing the privacy of her room before she burst into tears. Justin Lockwood had managed to ruin everything she'd worked for—again. He would do anything to increase his chances of winning, tossing integrity out the window.

Strike that—he didn't have any integrity to toss.

Three good cries later, Angela tossed her belongings in her suitcase. The sooner she left, the better, and not just because Grant suggested it. The last thing she wanted was to be there when the winner was announced tomorrow. Nor did she want to run into Justin and his gloating, hateful looks.

Angela got her lockbox down out of the closet, suddenly realizing Grace had the vial with her fragrance. By now, Grant might have it with the other entries since it was clear Grace hadn't known the truth of what was about to happen minutes after she walked away. As much as Angela wanted the sample back, she was more determined to leave.

It's not as if the sample would do anyone any good. No one could replicate the formula without her. She'd seen to that this time. If Grant had any proper sense of professional ethics, which she still believed he did, he'd return the sample, and he wouldn't even try to replicate it.

She managed to zip the suitcase after five tries, each effort hindered by excessive force. Glancing around the room to make sure she hadn't left anything, she headed for the door. It had been a rotten morning, but at least no one was around as she made her getaway. The last thing she wanted to do was answer questions.

Angela hefted the suitcase down the grand staircase, the heavy load making a thunking sound as the wheels landed on each carpeted step. Three steps to go, the wheels caught and hung. She yanked the suitcase, trying to pull it over whatever had snagged it, the motion sending her off balance. She reached for the rail, her hand missing, as she stumbled down a step.

"*Owww*," she howled as excruciating pain ripped across her ankle. She tried to grab the rail and pull herself up, but the pain was intolerable, reducing her to a heap of tears as she half sat, half lay on the step.

"Oh, this doesn't look good," Kyle said, glancing down at her, his eyes drifted to her ankle. "Let me help you." He offered his hand.

"It's no good, I tried. I can't put any weight on it," Angela said through her tears.

Kyle put a finger on his chin as he thought about the situation. "Hmmm, we've got to get you moved."

"What seems to be the problem?" Grant asked from above her.

She looked up to see him making his way down the steps. So much for a secret getaway.

"I think Angela may have sprained her ankle. Might be best if we get her back to her room and call the doctor," Kyle said, taking charge as he made a decision.

"Probably the best plan. I'll carry her back up the stairs," Grant said, moving past her.

"I don't think I need your help." There had to be a way to salvage some of her pride. She tried to pull herself up to prove her point, crumpling back down in pain.

"Quite the contrary. I think it's your only option." He leaned down and wrapped an arm under her legs and one around her back. "Hold on to my neck."

Angela ignored the order.

Step by step, Grant hauled her back to her room, Kyle following with her suitcase. Grant put her on the bed and headed straight for the door. "Kyle, get the doc here and be sure to bill it to Jaranda since she's still here under the terms of the competition." There was no kindness in his tone, though his offer was kind. And Angela was grateful she wouldn't have to foot the bill. It's not as if baristas were rolling in money—beans perhaps, but not dough.

"But why were you leaving? That's what I don't understand," Kyle asked, a confused expression on his face.

"I couldn't stay." It was the truth. A tiny piece of the truth, but still the truth, allowing her a small sliver of pride to remain intact.

"But the results are being announced tomorrow. Why would you leave before then?" Kyle's blank looked went back and forth between her and Grant.

Grant cleared his throat. "I guess it doesn't matter now. Get the doc and see what he says, as she may not be going anywhere." He turned and left without so much as a glance in her direction.

"I'll send for the doctor," Kyle said, trying to help her get comfortable on the bed and adjusting her pillows. "Hopefully, it won't take long. I'll get you some pain reliever in the meantime. Be right back." Kyle left, closing the door behind him.

Alone, Angela let the tears fall. Today was the worst day of her life. Between the disqualification, Grant's distrust, and now her ankle, the day was a close second to the day she lost her grandmother. As to the day she was fired from Contadine's, it slipped a notch or two. She cared far more about Grant's opinion, and the loss of his respect was a low point in her life.

The throbbing in her ankle had increased as did the swelling. She didn't need a doctor to tell her it was sprained, or that more than likely, she wasn't going anywhere today—or tomorrow, for that matter.

There was no way she could drive.

•♥•♥•♥•♥•♥•

"Please tell me you had nothing to do with that?" Captain Tremont frowned as he looked at Chloe.

She bristled at the question. "Of course not. Not everything that happens around here is because of me. I would never try to hurt anyone to make a match." Grant and Angela were proving far harder to bring together than she liked.

"Sorry, it's just that she was leaving, and..." The captain sent her one of his questioning looks

as if he still wasn't sure whether to believe her or not.

"Don't say it. It's not true. Honestly, I was at a loss. Clearly, providence stepped in to lend a helping hand, proof I'm right about those two. We just need to figure how to get them to see what's as plain as day. Grant's not trusting his own instincts."

"What if we locked them in the same room? Force them to communicate."

"Capital idea," Chloe said, nodding.

Chapter Eleven

CONFLICT FILLED GRANT, KNOWING Angela would be sticking around for a few more days. The fact he couldn't stop thinking about her or the situation wasn't helping. He couldn't have been more wrong about heaven-sent love, but at least he found out the truth before he made a fool of himself and the company.

Angela had deceived him, and he should have paid more attention to the warning signs. Like her perfume. He still didn't have answers as to why she'd still have *Rose d' Orange* and use it as a daily perfume—except today.

Today's fragrance was different. And although he loved *Rose d' Orange* on Angela's skin, today's scent was deeper, more luxurious. It created an elemental need to bask in the fragrance, to drink in the sweet and citrusy delicate notes. It was utterly unique and magnificent—and unlike anything he'd ever known.

Was it her entry to the contest? More than likely, and if not, it should have been. It was a masterful combination of essential oils, but there was the barest hint of a scent he couldn't isolate or identify. It made him all that much more curious about the fragrance because surprises were rare after twenty years in the business.

One thing that was for sure, if it had been her entry, he would have known it was hers. Is that why she wore it this morning? Even now, the fragrance lingered on his jacket. He didn't want to be suspicious, but how could he not? Angela, it seemed, was like his ex-wife with each new possible deception or hint of impropriety he discovered.

The only problem was the image he had of her all the other times. Like at dinner. Like when he watched her with the other entrants, laughing and carefree. Like during the garden tour. Most of the time, she came across as sweet and determined, a potent combination. It was the rest of the time that concerned him.

Which side of her was real? It didn't matter. After his VP had summed up the report, relaying the important information about Angela, the side of her that was deceptive was the only one that mattered.

In his room, Grant took the box with the samples from the finalists and sat on the couch, setting each one of the vials in front of him on the antique coffee table. His gaze kept drifting to the third vial, the one he needed to return to Angela. Grant resisted the temptation to open the vial and see if he'd been right and that she'd worn the fragrance entered in the contest. The underhandedness of such a bold move stuck in his gut like a knife.

Grant cleared his head, trying to focus on the two remaining bottles. One of them would be the new fragrance for Jaranda, or the basis for it anyway. He would never put out something he didn't consider perfect in every way. The contest had been to discover a new perfumer with a natural sense of artisan creativity.

His gaze drifted toward Angela's vial. She fit the bill, but integrity was crucial.

Returning his attention to the task at hand, he had to pick a winner. The brief had asked for entrants to create something vibrant, with long notes of floral that would cling to a woman's delicate skin. *Something unique*. He glanced at Angela's vial yet again, shaking his head.

Grant was almost positive it would hold perfection, but there was nothing he could do—or wanted to do. The reputation of the company wouldn't withstand a negative mark of this nature. Her past would checker the sales campaign, and he'd be the laughingstock of the industry.

One at a time, he tested the other two fragrances. It was a tough call, but in the end, he knew which one had to be the winner.

•♥•♥•♥•♥•♥•

The following morning, Grant went downstairs to the bistro. It wasn't long after that the press arrived to set up for the event. The three judges, David, and Justin, all arrived within minutes of each other, ready for the announcement when the time drew near. Grant didn't feel good about the decision, certain that the best of the three remained unopened in his room.

"I know you're all anxious to hear the results from the client. He made his decision this morning, and I'm here to present you with his pick for the winner of the brief.

As you know, you will work directly with the client, fine-tuning your sample to meet what the client envisions for a new signature fragrance. And, of course, the twenty-five-thousand-dollar prize." Grant nodded, looking around at each of the people in the room, focusing on the two remaining contestants.

"But shouldn't we wait for Angela?" Justin asked, a bit too self-satisfied for Grant's liking.

"That won't be necessary. Angela Bradbury has been...she was disqualified from the competition yesterday and won't be joining us." A general murmur of hushed voices rose in the silence of the bomb he'd dropped.

"Can you tell us why?" one reporter asked, the man doing his job and the question fully expected. *Just not one he wanted to answer.*

"No. Confidentiality rules prohibit the disclosure." And even if it wasn't true, he wouldn't have discussed it. What happened would remain between Angela, Alan, and Grant. And his VP understood the need to keep the information under wraps, for Jaranda's sake as well as Angela's. It was enough to have to disqualify her, but he wouldn't discredit her publicly as well.

"So, without further ado, the winner of the Jaranda Artisan Fragrance Competition is...Justin Lockwood for his sample of *La Bella.* Congratulations."

Justin was overly pleased with himself, his cocky attitude as he accepted the congratulations from the others not sitting well with Grant. But his sample was the best of the two. David, as expected, looked defeated. His entry had lots of potential but needed more work than Justin's.

Grant made a mental note to talk with the young man personally, to encourage him and let him know he was on the right track. He would also offer some suggestions for moving forward in his career. Grant shook hands with Justin and presented him with the oversized made-for-camera check. The real check would be mailed after Grant returned home in a few days.

He'd planned on going home this afternoon, but Angela's injury left him in a position where he didn't feel right leaving. She would need help, and he wanted to make sure she was taken care of, even if it meant he was the one to do it.

###

The day passed uneventfully after everyone left. Kyle continued to take care of Angela, just as he'd done yesterday. The inn was quiet, all the other guests having checked out as the celebrations ended.

By evening, Grant had come to a decision. It was silly to avoid Angela, given the circumstances. He headed for her room, a dinner tray in hand by way of a truce offering.

Knock. Knock.

"Come in," she called out, her voice gentle and with no evidence of her previous pain, the medication doing its job.

Grant entered the room. "I've got the chef's special you ordered for dinner." He shot her a smile, hoping she wouldn't throw it at the delivery guy.

"What happened to Kyle? You're the last person I expected to see here."

"Maybe so, but I'm here. I offered to give Kyle a break." He placed the tray across her lap when she sat upright, careful not to bump her ankle. "How's the injury?"

"Better thanks to some pain relievers and rest." Angela brushed her hair back from her face and looked over the tray of food, lifting one cover and then the next. "Doc says I have to stay off it for two days at the very least. Sorry, I know you wanted me out of here."

Grant shook his head. "It's all good. You need to rest and relax, and the Crestfield Inn is the perfect place to do it."

"Thanks for bringing my dinner. I'm sure you have plenty else to do this evening besides babysit."

"Sounds like you're trying to get rid of me."

"Well, we're not exactly in a good place," Angela said, frowning.

Grant could take a hint and the last thing he wanted to do was distress her further. "Okay, I'll leave. But only if you promise you'll call me if you need anything. After Kyle goes off duty, I prefer to know you're all right."

"I promise to call, but I'll be fine. It's not like there's much trouble I can get into."

Grant headed for the door. "Have a —" The door handle wouldn't turn.

"What is it, Grant?"

He glanced her way. "The, *ummm*, door seems to be stuck."

"So unlock it. We are the locking side." Angela frowned.

"Trust me, I would if I could—but it's not locked. It simply won't turn."

"That's odd. Maybe you could try jiggling it."

The medicine must be working well for Angela to tease him with his own words, even if they were said with disdain. "Old house, I guess. Let me call Kyle." Grant dialed and waited, crossing the room to the window to look outside. "Hey, Kyle. Angela Bradbury's door is stuck. She had some trouble with it before, and now the door won't open from the inside. The handle won't turn, and it's not locked."

"Hmmm. We've not had a problem with the handles before. I'll call in the maintenance man. Give him about twenty minutes, and he should be there. And I'll be back in an hour. There was no one checking in or expected, so I took advantage of the opportunity to run some errands."

Grant nodded. "I see. Okay. And I'll let Angela know."

"Thanks. Sorry about this. I can't imagine what's causing the problem," Kyle said before he hung up to call the repair guy.

"Let me know what?" Angela asked.

"They are going to send someone over to fix it. Should be about twenty minutes or so. Until then, I guess you're stuck with me. Sorry."

"Are you sure it's stuck? This isn't a ploy of yours to hang around longer?"

Grant frowned. "I'm not in the habit of being where I'm not wanted—so no."

"I never said you weren't wanted, just that we're in an awkward place."

"That's good to know. The others have all left, and I planned to stick around a few days to help you if needed. So it's good that you can tolerate my presence. Believe it or not, I feel awful for yesterday. It's not what I wanted to do, trust me. There was little choice in the matter." He moved to sit in the armchair and faced her. Grant missed talking to her, not as a perfumer—but as a person. More importantly, as his friend. If nothing else, he was being given a chance to make amends, if it were possible.

"Let's agree to disagree. Apparently, nothing can change the past. If you insist on helping, I don't want to discuss the competition. Agreed?" she asked.

At least she was willing to talk to him. It was a start. "Agreed." He nodded.

"One last thing on the subject before the subject is officially closed. Do you have my sample? I'd like it back." She leveled him with a determined look.

"I do, but I forgot to bring it with me." Another white lie. He'd been unwilling to give it up. When she left, it was the only thing he'd have to remember the perfection he associated with Angela. He only wanted a small amount, and then he planned to return the rest. The only issue was knowing it wouldn't have the delicate difference of Angela's skin to highlight the notes.

"I was surprised Grace accepted it until I realized you hadn't told her yet. Am I right?"

"No, I hadn't said a word. What transpired was between you and me." It suddenly hit him, the truth of Angela's words. Grace hadn't known because he hadn't told her. Angela was meeting Grace to turn the sample in—not him. He wasn't supposed to be there, which meant Angela wearing the fragrance was for no other reason than she wanted to. Knowing it wasn't meant to be a deceptive move put a huge chink in the armor he'd put up to isolate his feelings.

"Thank you. Did you eat already?" Angela asked.

"I did. Luckily, otherwise, you might be forced to share." He laughed. "You made an excellent choice. The *Coq au Vin* is beyond comparison," Grant said, relieved at the change in subject. Later, in the privacy of his own room, he'd sort out his conflicted thoughts.

Angela had accused him of not seeing beneath the surface, and he prided himself on doing just that, and he had with everyone—everyone except her, that is. Because if he looked beneath the surface with Angela, he knew what he saw. What he'd seen from the beginning—a lovely woman with a heart of gold. *Someone he could trust.*

He'd shoved what he knew about her aside, preferring to believe the bad because it was easier—easier not to address his feelings for her. But then there was the report his VP had relayed to him. It was black and white. Angela, aka Lindsay, had stolen someone's formula years ago, her intention to pass it off as her own. It was the kiss of death in this business—or any business, for that matter.

His heart couldn't risk another betrayal.

"Who says I would?" she teased, some of the Angela he'd come to know and appreciate returning. If only it could stay this way.

"You wound me," Grant said, placing a hand on his heart.

Conversation flowed, and before he knew it, thirty minutes had passed, and there was still no sign of the maintenance guy. Angela finished her dinner, and he moved the tray, placing it on the dresser.

"I thought the maintenance man would have been here by now," Angela said, glancing at her watch.

"Still looking to get rid of me, I see."

"No, we're fine. Really. I understand you did what you had to do. It's over and done and in the past. For me, the worst of it is..." Angela bit her lip, the words she'd been about to say left unsaid.

"Is..." he prompted her to continue.

"Nothing. Really." She turned and looked out toward the window, avoiding his gaze.

Knock. Knock.

Grant rose and made his way to the door. "Hello," he called out through the door, loud enough to be heard.

The door opened, and Grant stood back. "What was wrong with it?"

"Nothing, actually. I turned the handle and it opened. You know, the normal way."

The man grinned, trying to make light of the situation.

"I'll go out into the hall, and you see what happens from the inside. Just to be sure. I don't want Angela trapped in her room. That could be quite dangerous. Not that she can go far."

"Thanks, Grant." Angela frowned, shaking her head.

He moved into the hall to be on the safe side, preferring not to have all three of them locked inside. The maintenance man closed the door and then reopened it. "I don't know what to tell you, but it's working just fine."

"Okay. Thanks for coming out here." The man left, and Grant turned to Angela.

"Are you sure you weren't playing a prank so you could stay longer?"

"I promise you, I didn't. Scouts honor."

"Were you ever a scout?" she asked.

"No. But it sounded good." Grant chuckled. "Have a good night."

"You, too. And thanks for keeping me company tonight. I may not show my gratitude well, but your kindness is appreciated."

Grant left, feeling worse than he did before he arrived. She was nice...too nice to have done the things she'd been accused of.

What a conflicted mess.

"That went well," Chloe said, pleased with their efforts. Captain Tremont's idea to keep them locked in the same room had worked far better than when she had first tried. The captain had tricks up his sleeve he'd learned in the military, and they came in handy at times like this.

"Happy to be of service, my dear." Captain Tremont took her in his arms and twirled her about.

Chloe giggled. "Why Captain Tremont, you are such a flirt." She batted her eyes and waved her fan as if to cool her face.

"I think you're the flirt, acting all shy with your fan when you know you love me."

"That I do, Captain Tremont, that I do."

"Is someone here?" Angela asked, nervous trepidation lacing her voice as she glanced around the room.

Chloe and the captain paused, looking back and forth between Angela and each other.

"What do you make of that? I think she heard us," Chloe asked, moving closer to Angela.

"It's happened before when you make a connection, but that was a distant relative."

"Some people are more sensitive than others, almost like a gift. I knew I liked her right from the start."

"Maybe that's what draws you to people that you want to help find true love. An unexplained connection."

"You might be right, Captain. Just for fun, I want to try something." Chloe moved to the side of the bed and waved her fan in front of Angela.

Angela rubbed at her face. “Hello, is someone here?” she asked again, pulling the blanket up closer as if chilled.

“See, she senses our presence. This is wonderful. I mean, it’s not like I can just talk to her or anything, but it is very exciting to know people sense we are here. And I like that. A lot.”

The captain offered her his arm. “Shall we go upstairs, my dear? I believe you promised me a dance?”

“Just like every other night...the answer is always yes.”

Chapter Twelve

ANGELA HOBBLED FROM THE bed to the bathroom with the aid of the crutch Kyle had dropped off the first evening. The first rays of sunshine were coming through the window, casting a glow around the room. She glanced at her watch, quickly realizing she'd slept later than usual.

Crossing the room to the window, she peered out, watching as people bustled about on the street below. Life continued as normal for those around her, while her life had fallen apart. *Again*. There'd be no picking up the pieces and pushing to succeed. *This time, she was done.*

The industry was too small, and she'd been banned from it a long time ago.

It was unfortunate she was stuck at the inn for another day or so, knowing it would be easier to put all this behind her once she left here—and she *would* put it behind her. Giving up on perfuming didn't mean she couldn't enjoy the art of it for herself and her close friends. That was something no one could take from her.

It would also make it easier once there was some distance between her and Grant. Last night had been interesting. As much as she wanted to dislike him, she couldn't. He was only acting upon information he'd received. Grant had gone out of his way to take care of her, even making small talk while they waited for the maintenance guy to show up and fix a door that wasn't even broken.

And then there was the moment she felt someone was with her in the room last night after Grant left. A cold draft and a sensation of laughter had filled her. After lying awake for hours, she finally chalked it up to an old house filled with drafts and creaky noises—or vivid imagination.

Knock. Knock. "It's Kyle. I'm here with your breakfast. Is it all right to come in?" he called out from the hallway.

"Yes. Come in," she answered.

Kyle entered her room, his smile bright. "Good morning. I see everything is still working with your door."

"Yes, the man said there was nothing wrong with it. Odd to say the least."

"I'm glad to see you up and about. Don't overdo it unless you want to be laid up longer." His cheerful attitude always helped perk her up. It was hard to be disillusioned in the face of joy.

"Trying to get rid of me already?" she smiled. None of this was Kyle's fault, and after a day of recriminations and self-talking, she was ready to start over.

"You know better than that. Jaranda's picking up your tab, and I like the change of pace in helping you out instead of always being tied to the front desk. Not that I'd wish this upon you to make my life better." He winked, a teasing grin on his face.

"I knew they were paying for the doctor, but I didn't know Jaranda was paying for my extended stay. I would have thought they'd cut me off the minute I was disqualified."

"Mr. Edwards was adamant he was picking up the tab. Stay as long you like. We have plenty of availability at the inn this time of year." He waited for her to climb back in the bed before arranging the tray across her lap.

"This looks delicious," she said as he started pulling away the covers to reveal blueberry pancakes, sausage patties, fresh fruit, and pastries.

"Chef James put it together personally for you. Anything else you need?" Kyle asked as he poured her coffee.

"No, I'm good. Thanks. But ummm, Kyle, before you go, can I ask you something?" Part of Angela didn't want to ask, but the other part wouldn't let her not ask.

"Of course," he answered, pausing at the door.

"Who won the contest?" It was something she hadn't been willing to ask Grant last night when he'd dropped by to bring her dinner or during their conversation while locked in her room.

Kyle looked uncomfortable. "Justin Lockwood," he said, letting out a deep sigh.

Angela sucked in a deep breath, trying to keep her composure. It was nothing less than she expected, but still, the news was suffocating. *He'd won—again.* "Thanks for bringing me breakfast," Angela said, pasting a smile on her face.

Kyle waved and disappeared, the sound of the door closing like a signal to her brain. It was over. She closed her eyes, scrunching them tight to fight back against the tears.

This time Justin hadn't been able to steal her formula, but she knew now, without a doubt, he was the one who'd brought her past to the attention of the contest officials. Meaning, Grant Edwards.

Justin had warned her and then followed through. *Anything to win was his motto.*

She lifted the tray from her lap and set it aside, no longer hungry.

Part of what hurt was Grant's disapproving attitude towards her. She cared about him and had begun to think the feelings might be reciprocated. Instead, he'd believed the worst and hadn't bothered to ask her about any of it. And the knowledge he thought so poorly of her was the root of her discontent and the aching in her heart.

No one could take the art of perfuming from her whether she shared her skill with the world or not. But Justin had also managed to take Grant's friendship from her. The worst of it was that she hadn't even realized how much cared for him until now—when it was too late. Angela shook her head.

"I'd give anything for Grant to know the truth, but it's out of my hands. No one will believe me. They didn't four years ago, and they won't now. This isn't fair," she mumbled, resorting to talking to herself out of frustration with the turn of events and the knowledge she'd been powerless to stop it.

A cold draft passed over her. One of the floorboards creaked. It wasn't her imagination this time, but it was an old house. Angela shook her head, shaking off the odd sensation of being watched. She was alone in her room and letting herself get carried away at the slightest sound wasn't helping.

Chloe looked over at her handsome captain, her eyes filled with worry. "We have to find a way to help. It's clear she was falling in love with him. Why else would Grant Edward's opinion of her be more important than the competition? Locking them in together wasn't enough. We need to ramp this up a bit as we're running out of time. I just don't know what else to do."

"I do believe you are right, my dear. And you'll think of something. Your matchmaking gift hasn't failed you yet." He smiled at her, giving her the encouragement needed.

"Do you have any more ideas? Maybe we should continue to focus on Grant," she added, moving aside the bustle of her dress to sit daintily on the edge of the chair. It was a shame she hadn't been a part of a more futuristic era, the clothes of today looking far more comfortable than what she was resigned to wear for eternity.

Captain Tremont crossed the room and stood in front of the window, deep in thought. Suddenly, he turned to face her, a smile on his face. "I've got it. Why don't we make sure he learns the truth before he leaves? Sometimes, men can't see what's right in front of them when there are blinders in the way. I think the report from his VP is a blinder."

"But why would you think that? I'm not sure I follow." Chloe rose and went to stand by the captain.

He took her hand. "Let me ask you this. What do you believe about Angela? Do you think she's capable of stealing someone's formula?"

"Heavens, no. Just look at her. She's lost and moping and talking to herself about the truth. No regrets about what she did. The truth."

The captain nodded, his smile growing wider. "Exactly. I'm with you on this one. Which is why there must be more to the story. Something everyone is missing. I saw that Justin fellow talking to someone out on the front lawn the evening the message was delivered. Not saying he had anything to do with it, but it's all too convenient with the timing and the fact Justin won the competition. He had a lot at stake. Not to mention, I don't like the guy."

Chloe started, surprised at this latest information. "You didn't tell me about Justin talking to someone."

"You didn't ask. Would be hard to tell you everything, if I don't know what I'm looking for, my dear."

She nodded, realizing the truth of his words. "True. And I agree with you about Justin, but tell me—why don't you like the guy?"

Captain Tremont shrugged. "I pride myself on being a good judge of character, and I can see right through him. He's all charming on the outside and like a snake on the inside."

"That's what I thought, too. The question is, how do we get Grant to take a deeper look at Angela and push past the gray matter?"

"His employee summed up the details, and Grant didn't ask questions. He trusts his second in command, except there's more to the story. I feel it in my bones."

Chloe laughed. "You don't have any bones, silly man. But I think you may be right. There's more to the story, so the answer is to dig deeper. And I think you're a genius."

"How's that? I didn't come up with a plan, just why we need one." He stood by the window, arms crossed, one finger tapping against his arm.

"Actually, you did. It's just a matter of putting it all together. If we get Grant to dig deeper into the report, maybe he will see the truth." Chloe smiled.

"How do we do that? You heard her—no one listened before. Why would they now?" he asked.

"Because it's Grant—her soulmate. I just know I'm right about this." Chloe floated back and forth, pacing the room. "I've got it. Let's go to Grant's room and make sure he can't stop thinking about Angela. Her sample is in his room, and he hasn't opened it. But Angela has her own bottle, and she left it in the bathroom. What if we take hers and put some on his pillow? And on his towels. He did get a good whiff the day he disqualified her, and I can tell you, that man was smitten with the new fragrance. If he can't stop thinking of her, he will wonder why, and maybe we can find a way to point him in the right

direction. There has to be a way to cast doubt on what he heard and make him look deeper."

"I like it. And maybe while we are in Grant's room, something else will come to us."

"Come on, we've got no time to lose. She might leave tomorrow or the next day, and then we will have lost our chance."

Chapter Thirteen

PACING THE ROOM, GRANT stopped to look out over the gardens at the back of the inn. It was a view he normally enjoyed, but not this morning. Kyle had reassured him Angela was well taken care of and on the mend. Perhaps even able to leave tomorrow. Other than the one visit, Grant had stayed away. The memory of the time spent with her all too much of a reminder of the Angela he had thought he knew. The one he wanted to come to work for the company. The one he wanted to get to know better—on a personal level.

Unfortunately, staying away didn't get her out of his head. He hadn't touched her sample other than the once, and he certainly hadn't opened it, and yet two days later, he could still smell her, or the fragrance, that is, everywhere. It clung to his coat. It was in his bathroom. But worst of all, it stayed with him last night as he slept. Several times he woke up and found himself inhaling deeply, wanting more.

There was no way she'd been in his room, the steep stairs unmanageable for someone on crutches. There was no way to explain it, other than he simply couldn't get her out of his head. He knew she was crushed when he disqualified her, but what choice did he have? Grant had to think of the company and being associated with someone with her past attached, would close doors and send some of his perfumers packing for other companies.

His hands were tied, but even his dreams disagreed with the decision. Grant pondered the meaning of the dream and couldn't help but wonder if it was a subliminal message of some sort. He trusted Alan and his summation of what happened four years ago at Contadine Fragrances. Alan would have checked and rechecked the facts before reporting them to Grant.

He had to stop thinking he was the bad guy in all this. *Fair was fair.*

Except for the nagging doubt something was wrong stuck with him, just like her perfume stuck with him. Grant picked up the box that held her sample. The bottle was still signed and sealed, Angela Bradbury. More like Lindsey Bradbury. He preferred Angela, her sweetness like that of an angel.

Grant prided himself on being a good judge of character. Was it possible Angela had duped him? Or was there more to the situation that bore looking into?

Unable to resist, he opened the bottle, inhaling the instant release of floral fragrance that assailed him. It was like a summer breeze on an evening stroll, the citrusy orange spice hitting him first, followed by medium notes of a soft sweetness he couldn't identify. There was no doubt in his mind this was the perfume she'd worn the final day of the competition, the same one he couldn't get out of his head or his room.

It was a splendid creation of scent that lingered and charmed. Grant knew he would have declared it the winner of the competition and had zero reservations that he would have used it as the signature fragrance for Jaranda. *Without changing anything.*

It was exceptional—a masterpiece of a skilled artisan perfumer.

Angela Bradbury.

If she was this good without formal training or education, it could only mean one thing—she was a natural trained by another natural. The application listed her grandmother, leaving him to wonder who the grandmother might be. Angela's expertise clearly came from hand-me-down generational skills that typically surpassed all reasoning. And if he was right, she'd had no reason to steal someone's fragrance formula four years ago.

He needed to read the report Alan had gathered, hoping to glean some information that would be useful. The truth was important, and he planned to dig to the sordid bottom to find it out. Angela deserved that much from him.

He pulled out his phone and texted Alan.

Grant: Send me the entire report you drew up on Angela Bradbury. Following up on a hunch.

He didn't have to wait long before his phone chirped out a notification alerting him to an incoming text.

Alan: Will do. What's up? Sending to your email.

Grant: Thanks. Not sure, but something's not right.

Alan: Gotcha. Let me know. Your instincts have never failed you yet.

Except in this instance, his gut instinct may have kicked in too late.

Grant pulled up the email and downloaded the report Alan attached, as well as the article he'd found to support his investigation. Reading the report, he soon realized Alan had summarized everything correctly. There was nothing to be gained from the report itself. He clicked on the article. It was dated a little over four years ago and titled *'Contadine Employee Fired for Stealing Perfume Formula.'*

He read the article, word for word, hoping to gain a better insight into what happened. There wasn't much other than what Alan had already said until he reached the final paragraph. Grant's gaze landed on a name and stopped. He backed up and reread, paying closer attention.

Co-worker Justin Lockwood had turned the employee in when he discovered Bradbury's duplicity but was unavailable for comment.

Justin Lockwood—the same man he'd named winner of the Jaranda competition.

Angela and Justin had a past, and judging by Angela's reaction to the guy, not a favorable one. The question was, who should he believe? Because the article said one thing, but Grant was in favor of believing Angela. And not just because he cared about her. More so because she didn't come across as a liar or someone capable of deceit, unlike Justin.

He picked up his phone and searched for Brent Mateo's number. The perfume industry wasn't so big that he didn't know the top players. In fact, he and Brent had played golf together a time or two, and Grant was going to rely on that friendship now. As one of Contadine's top people, he would have the information Grant needed.

Brent answered on the first ring. "Grant, what a surprise."

"Hey there, sorry to call so early in the morning, but I need some information, and I was hoping you'd be able to help me out."

Grant paced the room, too keyed up with a need for the truth.

"You always were direct and to the point. What's up?" Brent asked.

"About four years ago, Contadine fired Lindsey Bradbury for stealing a formula from one of your perfumers with the intent to pass it off as her own."

"I remember it all too well. Totally unexpected turn of events, but there was nothing we could do about it," Brent said. "We found the formula in her possession, and it matched one of our perfumers' formula that he was entering in the company competition. Totally unexpected and such a shame. The girl had a lot of potential, which is why even as a novice, she was invited to submit."

Brent was confirming everything he already knew. He had to dig deeper. "I see. Any idea who trained her?"

"Her grandmother, of course. Why?"

Of course. Two simple words that held a wealth of meaning Grant didn't follow. "Who's her grandmother?"

"Isabella Fiora."

Grant frowned. *Isabella Fiora.* "I know that name, but why?"

"She was the leading perfumer at Balancia for years and renowned for her unique perfumes. She passed away about four years ago. I think I heard heart attack. The only good thing was that it happened before her granddaughter's downfall."

Grant knew exactly who the woman was now, the memory of her outstanding contributions to the perfume industry beyond compare. He'd never had the pleasure of meeting the woman, but she was an inspiration to many. "Can you tell me what happened at Contadine?" Now, more than ever, he believed there was more to the story. Isabella Fiora's granddaughter wouldn't need to steal a formula from a colleague.

"Why the interest?" Brent asked.

Grant tried to decide how much to share, not wanting to stir up trouble for Angela, but needing the truth. "Because an Angela Bradbury signed on as an entrant to the Jaranda competition I recently held for a client. But I recently discovered she'd changed her name to hide her past. Now, I'm trying to piece together what happened because, as you say, she's exceptionally talented, and I can't understand why she would need to resort to such tactics." He purposely left out the rest, not ready to reveal his suspicions.

"She's quite beautiful if I remember correctly. Anything to do with your interest?" Brent's question was an insult, or it should have been.

The problem was, Grant did find her beautiful, and he was interested, but it had nothing to do with why he was asking questions. "No. The truth is important. That's all."

"If you say so." Brent chuckled. "There's not much more to the story other than what I've told you, or that you probably read in the newspaper article written about it at the time. As a follow-up, however, Justin Lockwood, the beginner level perfumer who blew the whistle in the first place, did go on to win the competition. He was awarded a seat at the perfumer school in Paris, where he received full training in exchange for three years of being contracted with Contadine after his graduation from the program. He came back, and his first creation was a more refined version of his winning entry. The perfume released as *Rose d' Orange*. I'm sure you remember it. It was a big hit. Unfortunately, it didn't have the staying power because the middle notes dissipated far too quickly."

Far too many coincidences were popping up for Grant's liking. "I do remember it. I've smelled it recently and had trouble putting a name to it, although I remembered it was beautifully fragrant. Rather pleasant." Why would Angela still be wearing the perfume years later unless it was hers to begin with? It wouldn't have been a memory she would want to relive every day. There had to be more to it, and Grant was sure he was close to the truth. The fragrance had been hers.

"We ended production a year later, so it's doubtful someone still has any."

"It was similar, but not the same. Better, if you ask me," Grant said, trying to piece together the puzzle because one thing was for sure, the pieces weren't fitting together the way they were. Angela's original fragrance she'd worn the first couple of days was the result of a master at perfuming, not an inexperienced wannabe. "Do you remember why they decided Lindsey was in the wrong and fired her? Did anyone bother to consider Justin may have been the culprit?"

"I wasn't in charge of what happened in the investigation, but I do remember the discussions centering around her inexperience and status as a factory employee versus Justin having already worked there for over a year."

Circumstantial evidence. "Condemned without a fair hearing by the sounds of it."

"That may be true, but it was the only logical solution of how she got Justin's formula. You need to let this one go. If she's back in action, it's probably not good news," Brent said, trying to warn him off.

"Except she has natural perfuming skills that resemble her grandmothers, but Angela is also sweet, kind, and generous to a fault. And, I might add, she was only disqualified because someone made a point of revealing her past." He hadn't meant to admit to as much, but a part of him was trying to convince Brent of her innocence. It was important to him.

"Consider yourself lucky."

"I would if the person wasn't Justin Lockwood," Grant said, dropping the crucial piece of information that would throw a kink in the obvious.

"Justin?" Brent said, his tone far more interested than seconds before.

"Yes, he was one of the finalists with Angela Bradbury, and suddenly she's out of the running, smoothing the way for him to slide in as the client's favorite. Too much coincidence if you ask me."

There was silence at the other end of the line for an extended few seconds. "You might be right, Grant. Let me know what you find out and if I can help you in any other way. I hope we didn't do the girl a disservice years ago by putting our confidence in Justin."

"Me too, Brent. Thanks for your help." Hanging up, Grant was convinced Angela was on the up and up, and Justin was the culprit. The only thing left to do was prove it, and not only for Angela's sake. Grant didn't want to award the competition win

and the twenty-five-thousand-dollar check
to a loser.

Chapter Fourteen

POSITIVE HIS NEXT PHONE call wouldn't go as well, Grant looked up the number for Justin on his contest application and dialed it. He was more than ready to question Jaranda's winner.

"Hello?" Justin answered on the first ring.

"Grant Edwards. Of Jaranda Perfumes," he added for good measure.

"I know who you are. I just didn't recognize the number. What's up? Do you have a date when I can meet with the client or more information on what will happen with *La Bella*?" His voice carried a level of enthusiasm Grant wasn't sure he deserved, or that would continue when he learned the nature of the call.

"I don't have answers to either of those questions, but I do have a couple of questions for you," Grant said, eager to end the small talk.

"Okay, fire away." There was a little hesitation in Justin's voice this time.

"It's come to my attention that you were involved in an incident almost four years ago at Contadine, and I'm trying to get a better understanding of what really happened as it affected the outcome of Jaranda's recent competition. I'm vetting your background to make sure there are no unpleasant surprises for the client."

"Code for you talked with Lindsey Bradbury, and she gave you some mumbo jumbo sob story about me." Justin's friendly voice had taken on an edge Grant didn't care for. And he hadn't talked to Angela about what he'd discovered, but he planned on it. It would be better to play like he had, judging by Justin's attitude.

"Why don't you tell me your version of what happened? Just so I can be sure I picked the right person for the client, of course. I do find it odd the information was brought to my attention anonymously, and yet it involves you so heavily. I'm not convinced it was a coincidence."

Justin snorted. "I did what I needed to do to protect you and your company from making a mistake and naming someone with such an unsavory character as your winner. You should be thanking me." His tone had grown defensive, which was even more reason for Grant not to believe the man.

"And maybe I will be once I know the truth." *Unlikely, but he would be fair.*

"The truth is she stalked me. At first, I thought it was because she liked me, and then I found out it was the formula she was after all along. It came as quite a shock, and it broke my heart to discover I was played. I really liked her." Justin was over the top in his declaration, but of course, none of what he said could be verified. And neither did it change the outward appearance of the situation.

It wasn't enough for Grant. "Sorry to hear that. You did quite well for yourself with Contadine, but I noticed on your application you left about a year ago. What happened?"

"They happened. I'm not sure what their problem was, but I got tired of them passing me over. After *Rose d' Orange*, my first perfume for them, they never seemed to like what I did, always picking other fragrances to market. At the end of my three-year contract, I left. I'm better than what they wanted to give me credit for, and I wasn't willing to stay behind the scenes for long."

Grant was sure Justin was lying, but proving it wasn't going to be easy. The guy was good with his smooth answers. He glanced down at Justin's application. "And from there, you went to Tolstoy's. How's that going?"

"It's too soon to tell, but I think I've got a shot at next year's top formula. I'm hoping that collaborating with the client and getting credit for a new fragrance will push my name to the top of Tolstoy's list."

"Why do you think that?" Grant asked, pushing for more information. He wanted to understand how this guy thought and talking seemed to be his weakness.

"Because I'm good at what I do. Not to mention, they just lost their lead perfumer. Between you and me, I heard through the grapevine he was selling his formulas to another company and collecting a salary from Tolstoy's."

Overly confident and boastful, not a good combination. The man didn't have a speck of humility in him. "Sounds like he had a huge integrity problem."

"You could say that again." Justin snickered.

"So, tell me, how did you come up with *Rose d' Orange*, anyway? It's quite unique, even if lacking the middle notes for staying power. You did well with your first fragrance, if I remember correctly."

"I did. Made some good money." Justin hadn't answered his initial question.

"And how did you come up with the idea? It was genius for sure, although perhaps in need of more time to bring out deeper notes and refinement." The rush to put the fragrance out defied the rules of patience required in this business, categorizing Justin as the beginner he was, even after his training.

"I was just toying with different oils and combinations, and when I happened into that one, it stuck with me. I worked with it until I thought it was perfect while I was at school. *Rose d' Orange* was the result of a lot of trial and error, so to speak."

Error being the key word. Justin simply didn't have solid answers for anything, not to mention his key competition at Tolstoy's for the limelight, simply up and went rogue as a perfumer. How many times could Justin land on his feet without some behind-the-scenes action?

The third time would be his last if Grant was right about his gut feeling. And after hearing Justin's view on what happened with Angela, Grant's radar was echoing back at him from all four directions, and the waves didn't carry an ounce of good vibes.

Next stop, Angela Bradbury.

"Thanks for your time, Justin. And I'll be in touch about when the client wants to meet up. Take care, and good luck at Tolstoy's." Grant had a feeling Justin was going to need more than luck.

He was going to need an attorney.

###

Heading down the stairs, Grant's conscience made his steps feel twenty pounds heavier. It was as if he knew the truth before he talked to Angela. He still couldn't think of her as Lindsey Bradbury, preferring her angelic name. He hesitated in front of her door, trying to formulate his words.

Knock. Knock.

"Who is it?" Angela called out.

"Grant. I'd like to talk to you, please," he said, hoping she'd let him in for a visit.

"*Umm*, okay. Hold on a minute." Silence filled the hallways for what seemed an eternity before the door opened. "Sorry, it takes me a little bit to move around still."

"Thanks for talking to me. How is the ankle?" he asked, sincere in his concern.

"Better. I've talked to the doctor, and he thinks if I wrap it real tight, I might be able to drive. If I didn't drive a stick shift, there wouldn't be a problem. But seeing as that's not the case, I'm going to make a short trip in town to test the theory before taking the plunge to leave the inn altogether. I understand Jaranda's footing the bill and considering everything, it's very kind of you. Thank you." Her words only served to reinforce his opinion. Angela was a kind and sweet woman and not one capable of duplicity or evil. He'd made a huge mistake, and it was time to fix things. One step at a time.

He'd been played before and still needed solid proof. "It's the least we could do. I hope Kyle's taking good care of you."

"He is. The room has been a bit drafty the past couple of days, and he brought me more blankets. And he's kept me overloaded with some of the choicest selections from the chef's kitchen." The sight of Angela's smile had his heart doing flip-flops.

Grant moved further into the room, closing the distance between them. "That's great. Listen, the reason I stopped by was to ask you a few questions. I'm a little late in asking, but I hope you'll indulge me by answering."

Angela shrugged, looking more bewildered than ever. “I have no idea what you’re talking about, but I’ll do my best to help.” She crossed the room and sat in the armchair by the window. “Sorry, I need to stay off my foot to keep the throbbing under control.”

“No need to apologize. I realize my questions might upset you and that I’m breaking our agreement not to talk business. So, I’d like to apologize in advance.”

Her brow tightened, but she remained silent and waited.

“I want to ask you about what happened with Contadine.”

Angela let out a deep sigh, shaking her head. “I don’t—”

“Please, I want to hear what happened.” Grant moved closer but didn’t dare take her hand or force her to look at him. He had to keep her talking.

“Why?” she asked, leveling him with a hard gaze.

"Let's just say I've always been taught there are two sides to every story, and I want to hear yours."

Angela's chin rose a notch, although the twisting fingers in her lap gave notice to the uneasiness she was experiencing. "That's more than Contadine's wanted to know at the time, but I'm sure you've read the story in the paper."

Grant let out a deep breath. "That's not good enough. Not anymore."

"Have you talked to Justin?"

"I have." He wanted to be honest with her, trying to earn her confidence and trust.

Her face scrunched up in distaste as if his answer was like taking castor oil. "Let me guess, he said I pretended to love him and then used my relationship with him to steal his formula."

"How did you guess?" he asked, frowning down at her, more questions coming to mind with each comment Angela made.

Angela shrugged and shook her head. "Because it's what he did to me—not that anyone cares. It's bad enough to have to live with my own choices, so I'm not keen on touting my stupidity to the world."

"I care," Grant said, knowing it was true. He cared about a lot of things, many of them centered on Angela.

"Well, you're the first." She crossed her arms in front of her chest defensively.

"Tell me about the fragrance you were working on at the time all this happened?" he asked, pressing for more information. Somewhere in the story, there had to be something to prove her innocence.

"You mean the one he stole, changed a little bit, and then sold as *Rose d' Orange*?"

"Yes, that one." He grimaced.

"My grandmother and I worked on that together. It was our own special project, and we'd decided to enter it in the competition. I made the mistake of telling Justin about it, foolishly believing he cared about me. I learned my lesson not to trust anyone ever again. It's why I kept you at a distance. I didn't trust you."

Her comment stung, and it was something they needed to discuss later. But right now, he needed to stay focused. "You're talking about Isabella Fiora, am I right?"

"Yes, but how did you know? I purposely didn't put her name on the application."

"I've been doing some poking around and discovered a few things about you *and* Justin."

"Please don't put his name in the same sentence with mine. I've had more than my fill of his scheming lies ruining my life," Angela huffed.

"Then hopefully, you won't mind me asking about your fragrance. Am I right and that your formula is the one you wear every day?" He watched Angela closely for her reaction to the question.

"It is. I stopped working on it after my grandmother passed away, and then Contadine accused me of stealing the formula. I was distraught in dealing with my loss and didn't have the heart to fight Justin at Contadine. I'd just lost something way more important than a formula. My grandmother was the center of my life. And it's not like they would have ever believed a nobody like me anyway. By the time I recovered from my grief, it was too late and better to move on. In honor of my grandmother, I went back in and kept playing with the formula to make it better. It took a while, but I finally reached what I considered perfection. It's close to the original with some minor adjustments to help the middle and base notes stick out and last longer."

"Which is why you still have access to it. That explains a lot." He nodded. "How did you come up with the idea for the fragrance?" Grant asked the same question of Justin, but with Angela, he was sure he'd get a solid answer.

"We, Isabella and I, loved to play with the oils, combining some of our favorites. My favorite has always been orange, and hers was vanilla. Kind of like an orange sherbet ice cream bar." She smiled at the memory. "We decided to combine the two and then figure out what would work to take it from a childish fragrance to something like a summer's walk through an orchard and yet lasting long enough to go out on the town with more subtle notes."

"What do you call yours?"

"*Summer's Dream*." Angela said, the simplicity of the name making a strong impact.

"It's quite unique, and you wear it well. Much more subtle and lingering than *Rose d' Orange* ever possessed."

"Thank you. That's a wonderful compliment coming from you. But unfortunately, the outcome is still the same. I lose."

Grant shrugged, unwilling to commit to anything yet. "The sample you submitted—tell me about it. It too is unique, in a way that stays with a person long after you've left the room."

She glanced at him, a questioning look on her face.

"The day you turned the sample into Grace. You were wearing it."

"I was, but I wasn't expecting to run into you, otherwise, I would have never been so daring. It would have come across as wrong—almost manipulative." Grant had figured as much and believed her.

"The fragrance stuck with me long after you went to your rooms. I couldn't get it out of my head. Trust me, I tried. Enough so that I've opened your sample to have the pleasure of it once again." He wouldn't go so far as to tell her how it pervaded his room, and his memory in overtime.

"I call it *Isabella's Honey Angel*. She taught me everything she knew and gave me the olfactory gift of insight. We had an idea that if we came up with the perfect rose, we could make the perfect scent. She passed away on the third-generation plant, but I continued working on it the past few years. It's the basis for the fragrance." Angela's animation levels increased as she spoke of the rose and her grandmother, her face flushed a pretty pink.

"Which explains why I couldn't place the rose scent. I'd love to see the flowering plant someday." A novice perfumer wouldn't have been able to accomplish all that Angela had, her creativity more natural, like that of grandmothers.

"You would?" she asked, clearly shocked by his request.

It was time to let her know what he was thinking and that he believed in her. "Angela, you need to understand my position as the head of Jaranda. I had to cover the PR bases and respond to a potentially damaging report. I do feel there's more to the story, and I'm sorry if I had to make a spontaneous decision that hurt you. But that doesn't mean I'm convinced you're a bad person capable of the charges brought against you. In fact, I feel quite the opposite, which is why I want to help."

"It's too late to help. The damage has already been done. Twice. History repeated itself." Her smile slipped from her face, and Grant vowed to make things right.

"What do you mean?" he asked.

"Justin threatened to expose my past if I finaled. He would do anything to win, no matter who he hurts in the process."

"Do you have any proof of those threats?" Grant kneeled next to her and took her hands in his.

"No. He's smarter than that."

"He might not be as smart as you think," Grant said, smiling. There was another avenue he wanted to check out, one that might finally put an end to Justin's treachery.

"What's that supposed to mean?"

"If my suspicions are right, I'll tell you later. Please don't leave the inn just yet, not until I have time to check into something. Trust me on this, please."

"Okay." She nodded, looking unsure even as she replied.

"Promise?" he asked. Grant didn't want her disappearing out of his life. There had to be more to whatever was between them, but first, he had to lay her past to rest.

"I promise."

Grant nodded. He believed her promise, which would buy him some time. The last thing he wanted to do was get her hopes up for nothing, but by the end of the day, he wanted answers—one way or the other.

Chapter Fifteen

KNOCK. KNOCK.

Angela turned away from the window to glance at the door. Kyle had already brought her breakfast, and the only other person who visited was Grant. She was betting on the latter, and her heart agreed, the sudden staccato rhythm pounding in her chest. She'd hadn't heard from him since yesterday's conversation, one that left her breathless with hope.

"Come in," she called out, not bothering to cross the room just to open the door. Her visitor could do it as well as she could.

Grant entered, a smile on his face. "Good morning. Did you sleep well?"

Odd question given the situation between them, his nonchalant, chipper attitude filling the room. It was hard to ignore, her sense of good news on the horizon making her heart race. "Good morning. And not overly, but I'm fine."

"Good, good. I'm glad to see you dressed already, as that makes things a bit easier."

He was babbling on, not making any sense. Angela had a feeling she could have told him she didn't sleep a wink and he would have thought it good. "Easier for what?"

"To go downstairs, of course. Didn't Kyle get you the message?"

"No message." She glanced at the untouched breakfast tray on her bed. Angela hadn't been overly hungry and opted to shower instead, a process that took far longer than normal with her ankle issue. It turned out to be more like a sit-on-the-edge-of-the-tub shower. A chilling experience for sure.

Grant's gaze flicked to the tray before he grabbed the folded white note and held it up. "This message," he said, a wide grin on his face. "It says to be ready by nine a.m. for an important meeting. Mandatory attendance. Good thing you're showered and look ready to face the world. I would have hated to carry you downstairs in your pajamas." He winked.

"Slow down. Why would I go to a meeting I know nothing about, and why would I let you carry me there?" He was going too fast, not to mention, she wanted to know what the fuss was all about. If he had good news...

"Because you want to be there, and I'm the best ride in town." Grant was almost laughing at her, his efforts to hold back all too obvious.

"What's the meeting about?" she asked, hoping for a hint.

"Maybe we can go downstairs, and then you'll find out." Grant crossed the room to her side and held his hand out for the crutches.

It didn't seem like she had much choice, not to mention her curiosity had kicked into high gear. Being this close to Grant sent shivers of awareness down her spine, his cologne having a powerful effect on her senses. The woodsy tones on his skin were a perfect match. "I can walk," she said, thinking it a safer option.

"You could, and you might fall going down the stairs. My arms are much safer. Trust me." It was hard to resist Grant when he was this charming.

"Fine." She handed him the crutches, which he leaned against the wall.

Grant gazed down at her, unmoving. "It's all good, so relax."

She believed him. Still, he didn't move, her skin flushing as he continued to focus on her. "What's wrong? Is there something on my face?" she asked.

He shook his head. "Only this." Except instead of brushing something away with his fingers, his palm cupped the side of her cheek, and he lowered his head to kiss her.

The effect was dizzying. Enough so, she allowed herself to enjoy the moment, even joining in, instead of pulling away the way she should have.

All too soon, he pulled back and scooped her in his arms, pulling her in tight against his chest. "That was nice," Grant said, his voice deep and gravelly.

Nice? That's all he thought of the kiss, when to her, it was mind-numbing perfection. "Yes." She wasn't about to give him a higher rating than he gave it, even if it was true. And more importantly, why had he kissed her? That's what she really wanted to know but refused to ask. She'd find out what he was up to soon enough.

Grant carried her into the bistro, where they were greeted by lots of people—the press included. They were quick to start taking pictures of her in his arms, and she struggled to get down.

"Hang on, you have a front-row seat to this meeting," he murmured close to her ear, his breath sending a fresh wave of chills down her spine.

"Grant—"

"You'll see." He lowered her to the seat before moving to stand in front of the group.

Angela looked around the room but didn't recognize any of the people. Almost everyone had badges as if they were all reporters, which didn't make any sense. She spotted Kyle off to the side and waved, thankful for a friendly face.

"Good morning, everyone. Thank you for coming here on such short notice. Most of you were here for the announcement of the winner of Jaranda's recent competition. I promised if you showed up this morning, today's announcement would make your effort worthwhile. So, without further ado, as the sole owner of Jaranda Perfumes, I'd like to officially go on the record with a retraction of the previous winner, Justin Lockwood." Grant shot her a look, his warm smile giving her pause.

Angela sucked in a deep breath, her head spinning. What did he mean? Adrenaline raced through her body, goosebumps appearing on her arms.

The crowd's in-drawn breaths and murmurings echoed her surprise.

Grant held up his hand for silence. "It has come to my attention that Mr. Lockwood is of dubious character and has acted in malice on several occasions to change the outcome of this competition and other situations. Previously, Miss Angela Bradbury was disqualified from the competition because of information received by Mr. Lockwood. The information was found to be falsified, and it is with the deepest regret

I allowed myself to act upon it. Therefore, I'm reinstating Miss Bradbury in the competition and announcing her as the winner. Her sample was beyond comparison, and the client wishes to begin production of *Isabella's Honey Angel* as a signature fragrance at once."

Angela couldn't believe it. Her prayers had been answered, in God's time, not her own. Tears filled her eyes. Grant just announced her as the winner, and her fragrance would be sold worldwide. It was a dream come true. Later, she'd have to ask him how he found out, but right now, she wanted to enjoy the moment.

Justin had finally gotten his comeuppance.

Grant gave her his hand and pulled her up. They stood side by side as photographers rattled off questions and took pictures. Angela beamed, answering the ones directed at her and letting Grant field the more inquisitive ones about Justin—to which he typically answered, no comment.

•♥•♥•♥•♥•♥•

Grant felt relieved as the last of the reporters left. Although frustrated by his *no comment* reply when it came to Justin Lockwood, they were satisfied having the scoop on an exceptional story that would break immediately.

Angela had been a joy to watch as the truth was revealed and as the realization she'd won set in. Now, all that was left were the personal explanations, the ones for her ears only.

"That was fun," she said, grinning as he approached. In the space of thirty minutes, the Angela he'd come to know had returned, her joy of life evident in her every move.

"And deserved." He nodded.

"What happened? This was a major bombshell, even if a good one."

"We can talk upstairs—privately." Grant swooped her up in his arms, something he was enjoying far too much. Earlier, he hadn't been able to resist kissing her. And when she'd kissed him back, he knew there was still a chance for the two of them and that he hadn't ruined everything. But he wouldn't push his luck. Not yet anyway. Time and place were important.

"You plan on making a habit of this?" She laughed.

"When necessary." Secretly he hoped it would be necessary, but not for the same reason. Grant carried Angela up the stairs, enjoying her closeness, and the trust she placed in him. She pushed open the door, and he set her down on the edge of the bed before returning to close the door.

"We are as private as we can get, so spill the beans, mister." Angela smiled, her cheeks dimpling.

Grant sat in the chair nearby. “First, I’m truly sorry I didn’t dig beneath the surface before I reacted. There wasn’t time, and I was sure Contadine wouldn’t have acted without cause. I was wrong. They reacted with the appearance of events, not facts.”

“But how do—”

“I know because I called them. I’ve got friends in this business. Turns out it was based entirely on Justin’s side of the story, just like you said. And since you never contradicted his claims, they assumed you were guilty and all too happy to leave. It was the easy way out of a messy situation. It’s what started me to question people, including you and Justin.”

“My grandmother passed away. Something far more important to me at the time than Justin’s lies and deceit.”

“I understand that now. Fast forward to Jaranda’s competition. After everything that happened, I couldn’t get you or your fragrance out of my head. It’s as though you were in the room with me no matter what I did. I realized the quality of the fragrance you wore was far superior to Justin's *Rose d' Orange*. It made no sense if you were inexperienced and without training to be able to create a scent that stayed with a person long after they left the room. Like a memory." Grant took her hand, bringing it to his lips for a gentle kiss.

Angela blushed, her radiance like the sun. "Like I mentioned before, the formula he stole wasn't finished. It took another year to perfect the fragrance to my satisfaction."

"Your dedication shows, trusts me. And you were right. Your finished product was far superior to his." It was one of the things that had given him pause earlier on. Justin's scent was beautiful, but not lasting. On Angela it was exquisite. To a trained perfumer, he should have realized the subtle difference was more than a simple reaction to the person who wore it.

"What happened after that?" Angela asked, urging him to continue.

"When I called Justin and confronted him on the issue, he made a huge mistake in assuming you'd ratted him out and began spinning his own tale, but knowing you the way I do, it still didn't add up."

"Thank you for that, believing in me. It means a lot," Angela said.

"I'm just sorry I ever doubted your integrity. In time, I hope you'll forgive me."

"Finish the story of what happened, and I'll consider it," she teased, giving him the confidence she'd already done just that—forgiven him. It was more than he deserved, but it didn't stop him from wanting it.

"Justin buried himself, so to speak. He was in a bragging mood and referred to one of Tolstoy's perfumers who was fired for selling formulas to another company while accepting the salary from Tolstoy."

"But why—"

"That's what I wondered, so I did some more digging. I made a call to another friend of mine at Tolstoy, and all sorts of warning bells went off. I spent most of the night on the phone with the owner of Tolstoy and investigators. They tapped into his work computer and company phone records, and it seems Justin was the one selling formulas he was stealing from the other employees. He even went so far as to buy a flashy car after the employee was fired.

"The investigators got a warrant and were able to quickly trace the wire transfer of funds to his account from another company. The reason I didn't want to say anything to the reporters was that I didn't want to tip Justin off before the authorities moved in to arrest him. He's got a lot bigger problems than being disqualified from Jaranda. I think it's safe to say Justin Lockwood will never darken Jaranda's doorstep again. Or yours."

Angela let out a deep breath. “Finally. It’s over. I shouldn’t be happy, but I am. He’s ruined my career and deserves what’s coming to him for all the misery he’s caused others.” She stood, reaching for Grant’s arm. “Thank you. For everything.”

He took her hands and drew them to his chest, moving her closer. “I wouldn’t say he’s ruined your career. In fact, I’m hoping this is just the beginning.”

“What do you mean?” she asked, her gaze going to their hands he held trapped. Her flushed face was radiant in the morning light.

Grant smiled and nodded. “I’d like you to come to Jaranda and tour the company. See if you like it there, and then we can talk about you joining the team.” There was more to his request, but this was a good place to start.

“I’d love to visit. But I’m not sure joining your team is what I want for my future though. It’s a great opportunity, but with the money from the prize, I'd planned on opening my own store and doing my own personal fragrances. A select boutique of sorts. I'm sorry, but I don't think I could handle another setback. I need security." Angela pulled her hands free, putting distance between them.

"Well then, hopefully before you leave Jaranda, I can change your mind." Grant wasn't giving up yet, not by a long shot. This was about way more than gaining an employee. This was about renewed life and trust and the future.

"We did it," Chloe said, grinning as she watched the pair finally connect. Angela was too much in love to let this opportunity slip away. She simply needed a little extra time, and after all the poor girl had been through to get to this point—she deserved happiness.

"I must say, you were right again, my dear. Although technically they are leaving, and we won't know if they ever get together." Captain Tremont slid an arm around her, drawing her in close.

"That's where you're wrong. We do know. Because we know what love looks and feels like, and they both have it in hearts and roses. Literally." She laughed at her own joke.

He pulled her toward the window. "See that spot down there," he pointed toward the rose garden at the back of the inn, a small path that wove through the bushes that led to an alcove.

"Yes," she said, glancing up at him, wondering where this was leading.

"That's where I first saw you. My hearts and roses moment. Unfortunately, I got mixed up between you and your sister."

"Twin sister, so you're forgiven. I say we go down to your spot and celebrate another matchmaking success."

"Lead on, my dear. My heart will always follow yours for eternity."

Chloe took one last look at the happy couple. They might not know what lay ahead for them, but this is what life as she knew it was all about. Correction, life as she and the Honorable Captain Tremont knew it. Life was about love.

Chapter Sixteen

THE FLIGHT TO BURLINGTON only took two hours, but it was a most enjoyable flight for Angela. First class. Grant was going overboard to make amends for disqualifying her, even though she'd told him repeatedly she didn't blame him. Never had.

Well, for one little bit she had, knowing he'd made his decision without talking to her. But then, the article said more than enough. What bothered her the most was the loss of respect she'd seen in his eyes and knowing the short but sweet friendship they'd shared was over.

Her grandmother would have been thrilled with the turn of events, and Angela felt her presence every step of the way this past week as she prepared to tour Jaranda.

She'd received a contract from the client for *Isabella's Honey Angel.* Grant wanted her to have an attorney look it over before the client's name was revealed. The terms were more than generous and far beyond her wildest dreams. The prize money was safely in her bank account, but the advance offered for the fragrance was four times the amount. All she had to do was sign on the dotted line.

She trusted Grant. As far as she was concerned, an attorney wasn't necessary.

Passing through the gate into the waiting area after deplaning, she was plenty surprised to see Grant waiting for her. A flush of pleasure raced through her, his warm smile welcoming.

"Good afternoon, Angela. I trust you had a nice flight," he asked.

"Hello to you, too. I did, thanks to you." Angela pushed her purse out of the way and leaned in to hug him. He had kissed her once upon a time, so it was only fitting.

Grant's arms came around her, and all at once, she had a sense of coming home. "You wore my second favorite perfume, and it's heavenly on you."

"Second favorite?"

"*Isabella's Honey Angel* is my new favorite. The uniqueness of the rose blossoms add an unforgettable elegance that mixes with the base note of patchouli in a way the notes stay with a person long after the wearer has left the room."

"What a beautiful thing to say." It was no wonder she'd fallen in love with him. He understood her, and he believed in her. It would make it that much harder to leave in a couple of days. She promised him she'd tour the company, but after that, nothing had changed. Her shop was her future and her security.

"For a beautiful person, inside and out. I just wish—"

"Grant, you have to stop beating yourself up over this. It ended well. Promise me, no more apologies."

"I promise. My driver is waiting to take us to Jaranda. Shall we?" He indicated which way to go with a wave of his hand, picking up her bag to carry.

"Works for me. I can't wait to see everything."

###

Twenty minutes later, they pulled up in front of a windowed building laid out like a semi-circle. It was more modern than Angela would have expected. And larger. "It's gorgeous. Did you design this?"

"No, I can't take the credit. My father did after the original Jaranda warehouse became too small for the company. My grandfather started the business, but it was the two of them working together that made the company what it is today."

"I'm sure you've had your hand in it. You don't seem to be the sit back and let it happen kind of guy." Angela smiled, remembering how he'd been determined to learn the truth about her and right the wrongs Justin had perpetrated.

"Okay, so maybe a little." He winked.

Grant introduced her to a few people as he led her around the building, explaining what area they were in and the importance. But it was the creation rooms that intrigued her the most. Ultramodern equipment and large desks, each filled with hundreds of vials of oils holding every scent imaginable were at the perfumer's disposal. Each room was enclosed in glass to keep the fragrances pure as they were mixed and aerated, but the glass gave the sense of light, airy, and huge. Like they were all part of one big family. Even the peach and light blue walls were artistically painted, leaving one with a sense of peace. A creator's dream environment.

He turned to her and smiled. "What do you think? I saved the best for last, knowing this would be your favorite."

"You were right. This is amazing." Angela walked around the room, unable to resist reaching out and trailing her fingers across the desk.

"Amazing enough for you to join the team?" he asked, stepping to one side.

She spotted her name engraved on a plate with the words Junior Perfumer underneath. The job offer was official. He'd warned her he would try and convince her. She hadn't expected to fall in love with the place or the man, making her rejection almost impossible.

The problem, however, was trusting someone else. What if something else happened and she found herself at the exit door? Angela wanted to trust him, but still, she hesitated. Searching for a way to let him down gently, she focused on the fragrance contract in her purse. "But what about the client? I've got to work with him, and I'm not sure how long that will take. I mean, this is amazing, but I'm not sure legally what my options are at this point." She was stalling, but it couldn't be helped.

Angela wanted to say yes, but there was too much of her past to overcome.

"Did you have an attorney look over the contract?" he asked.

"I didn't. I don't have to because I trust you." She pulled the envelope out of her bag and handed it to him. "It's signed."

Grant's smile widened as if she'd given him a gift. "Wonderful news—and it's also the answer to your question. You see, the thing is..." He took her by the hand and pulled her close.

She'd never seen him at a loss for words. If it wasn't for his smile moments ago, she'd have been worried. "What is it? Is there something wrong?"

"The thing is, if you agreed to the contract, then you've agreed to work with me. I'm the client."

Grant? She shook her head, trying to piece together this last tidbit of information with all that had happened. “You? But you said—”

“I’m sorry. I wasn’t at liberty to tell you.” Grant said, taking her hand in his. “And I never actually lied—I just side-stepped your questions.”

Angela frowned. “I’m not sure I agree. You told me you weren’t judging.”

“What I said was I had nothing to do with picking the finalists. And I didn’t.”

“Splitting hairs. Oh, this is bad. Did you pick me as the winner because of this…” she pointed a finger back and forth between them, “this attraction between us?” Angela wanted no part of deceit and lies; she’d had enough of that to last a lifetime.

“First, I’m glad you noticed and can admit to the attraction. I was beginning to think I was the only one. And second, to answer your question—no. I picked *Isabella’s Honey Angel* because it was the clear winner from the start. From the minute I breathed in its very essence when you wore it, I knew it was unforgettable. It's why I want it to be the new signature fragrance of Jaranda. The one to take this company into the next decade. It's also why I offered you such a large advance and a percentage. This fragrance will be timeless," Grant said, his voice filled with sincerity.

Angela wanted to believe him. "You really think so?"

"I know so." He nodded.

The job offer didn't guarantee her future, but Grant offering her a piece of the signature fragrance of Jaranda, well, that was financial security. She wanted to stay, and he was making it possible. Perhaps in time, they might even figure out what to do with the feelings they clearly shared with each other. "Then in that case, I accept your offer of employment." She nodded.

"There's one other thing."

"Oh, what's that?" she asked, not liking the idea of conditions.

"I'd like to offer you the official position as my girlfriend, and hopefully, one day, my wife. You see, what I feel for you goes way beyond attraction. I'm in love with you."

Angela's heart raced as she threw herself into his arms yet again. "Yes and yes. I accept both titles, Junior perfumer and girlfriend. I love you, too. I kept hoping in time you'd consider something beyond friendship. I can't believe you feel the same way. You don't think it will look bad, do you? I don't want everyone to think I'm getting special treatment."

"Actually, that's why I'm starting you out as a junior perfumer. Right alongside David, who, by the way, starts work next Monday." Angela's heart burst with love for Grant. He was a good man. *Her man.*

"That's wonderful news. You're the best," she said, laughing, as she thread her arms around his neck.

"As long as you only have eyes for me," Grant winked.

"Naturally." She grinned.

"You know, even if you hadn't agreed to sell Jaranda complete rights to the formula, I would have still wanted you in my life. Love is more important than anything, including the fragrance."

"I couldn't agree with you more, boss," she teased.

Grant had thought of everything. By starting out as a junior perfumer, she'd have a chance to work her way up and gain the respect of the other employees. It didn't matter what her title was if she had Grant—a man who was always fair, and just, and the kind of person she could believe in. *Forever.* The kind of man her grandmother would have wanted for her. He'd been as elusive as her *Isabella's Honey Angel,* but worth waiting for.

"To seal the deal," he murmured, leaning in to capture her mouth for a special magical kiss—the toe-curling kind.

The sound of clapping erupted from the hallway. Clearly, there was one disadvantage to glass walls, not that she minded. Grant Edwards loved her, and she wanted the whole world to know she loved him right back.

What to read next...

If you loved this story, be sure to check out book 3...
Turning Down Pie
Recovering from an injury, the last thing she needs is the media limelight. Or a handsome avalanche flattening her on the ski slopes. Pick up a copy of
Turning Down Pie
to find out what happens...

The greatest compliment you could give

an author is to leave a review in order to help other readers discover the same great stories you enjoyed. Amazon/Bookbub/Goodreads are all great places. Many thanks!!!

Want to keep in touch with new releases and what's happening in the world of Elsie Davis? *Sign up for the monthly newsletter here... Elsie Davis HEA* (Happily-Ever-After) And while you're there, be sure to check out the new Elsie Davis Bookstore where you can buy books direct at discounted prices.

Another great way to keep in touch - ***Follow Elsie Davis on FaceBook***

Also By Elsie Davis

Sweet, Clean and Wholesome Stories...with a Happily-Ever-After Guarantee!

Holidays in Hallbrook

(Sweet Romance Series for Holidays Throughout the Year)

Welcome to Hallbrook, New Hampshire. A small-town filled with the unexpected, lots of love, and of course, a beloved dog to ramp up the excitement.

Love & Order (Labor Day)
Love & Family (Thanksgiving)
Love & Peace (Christmas)
Love & Chocolate (Valentine's Day)
Love & Hope (Mother's Day)

Love & Liberty (Independence Day)
Love & Honor (Veteran's Day)
Love & Joy (Easter)
Love & Adventure (Father's Day)

Great Smoky Mountain Getaways
(Christian Inspirational – Women's Fiction Romances)
Juliet's Journey to Love
Poppy's Path to Love
Rachel's Road to Love

Crossroads Creek Cowboys
(Christian Inspirational Romances)
The Heart of a Cowboy
The Help of a Cowboy
The Return of a Cowboy
Coming Soon – The Care of a Cowboy

Crestfield Inn Romances

If you like special kinds of soulmates, a splash of the supernatural, and wholesome relationships, you'll adore this sweet bit of fun filled with romance and mystery.

Turning Back Time

Turning Up Roses

Turning Down Pie

Celebrity Corgi Romance

(Standalone Sweet Romance)

If you like light mystery mixed in with your happily-ever-after, you'll enjoy this second-chance romance and the race to save an adorable Corgi.

Digging the Driver

Gold Coast Retrievers

(Sweet Romance)

Special Golden Retrievers help their humans solve mysteries, save lives, and even find love...

Defending Dakota

Trinity River

(Sweet Western Romance)

Ranchers and farmers depend on the Trinity River for water, but when a secret conglomerate starts buying up property by fair means or foul, it's time for the landowners of Tumble County to fight back—Texas style. But what they don't count on, is finding love in the process.

Back in the Rancher's Arms

Small Town, Big Secrets

Coming Soon! (2023-2024)

Sundancer's Legacy – 9 Book series

Sundancer's Star

Sundancer's Joy

Sundancer's Heart
Sundancer's Majesty
Sundancer's Miracle
Sundancer's Glory
Sundancer's Kiss
Sundancer's Moon
Sundancer's Splendor

About The Author

Elsie Davis is a *USA Today and International Bestselling Author* of over 25 sweet, clean, and wholesome romances, and a member of the ACFW. She discovered the world of Happily-Ever-After romance at the age of twelve when she began avidly reading Barbara Cartland, the Queen of Romance, and has been hooked ever since. After building her dream log home on top of a small mountain, she turned her attention to do what she loves most, writing. Elsie writes sweet Contemporary Romance and Contemporary Christian Romance from her heart...hoping to share a little love in a big world.

When she's not writing, she can be found birding, kayaking, camping, fishing, playing disc golf, and taking nature walks—hoping to spot wildlife. Basically, she loves all things outdoors, EXCEPT cold weather. She and her husband are avid Caribbean cruisers, but Elsie's favorite vacation was their cruise to Alaska. (In spite of the cold!) Indoors, she enjoys a toasty fire, and of course, a great romance with a guaranteed Happily-Ever-After.

https://www.elsiedavishea.com

www.ingramcontent.com/pod-product-compliance
Lightning Source LLC
Chambersburg PA
CBHW020104310726
48970CB00002B/468
* 9 7 9 8 9 8 6 1 1 7 7 2 0 *